A.C. PAPA
Number One, 2015

First Printing: January 2015

ISBN: 978-1-312-60735-4

Poet Plant Press
Saint Augustine, Florida 32086
www.bodor.org

Also by Poetnoise/ Poet Plant Press:

Train of Thought (1996)
Alt Dot Spoken Word (1997)
Poetnoise 2000 (2000)
My Time-The Lunch Break Book (2007)
Employees Only-The Work Book (2009)
Heart Pour-The Love Book (2011)
Florida Speaks (2014)

The next reading period for Ancient City Poets, Authors, Photographers & Artists (A.C. PAPA) will be May 01, 2015 to July 31. The focus of this Saint Augustine based journal is to spotlight Florida artists and art that references the Sunshine State. We will accept submissions of poetry, fiction, fine art and photography. A.C. PAPA is looking for writing and artwork that speaks of Florida, from all angles and all perspectives. We would like to hear from locals, tourists, travelers and residents. A.C. PAPA will appear each January, featuring the best work from Florida artists as well as national and international writers who have something to say about Florida. All are invited to submit image and word submissions by email, as an attachment, to acpapalitmag@gmail.com.

ANCIENT CITY POETS, AUTHORS, PHOTOGRAPERS and ARTISTS

EDITOR-IN-CHIEF
Chris Bodor

EDITORIAL BOARD
Mary Beth Bodor, Charlie Cawley, Leny Kaltenekker,
Kimmy Van Kooten, Michael Henry Lee, Robert Waldner

FRONT COVER PHOTO BY
Mark Kirwan

ADDITIONAL FINE ART AND PHOTGRAPHY BY
Alex Boardman, Brian Druggan, Dan Florez, Marie Groves,
LeeAnn Kendall, Rhiannon Lee, Rebecca Rousseau

PUBLISHED BY
Poet Plant Press
Saint Augustine, FL 32086
poetplantpress@yahoo.com
www.bodor.org

"I am the lizard king, I can do anything."

—Jim Morrison

"I ain't the world's best writer nor the world's best speller,
but when I believe in something I'm the loudest yeller."

—"Stetson Kennedy" by Woody Guthrie

"During the late 1950's Jack Kerouac lived just northwest of downtown Orlando, on a quiet street in a College Park neighborhood, not much different from mine. He spent many a humid Florida night toiling away until dawn working on his book **The Dharma Bums**, one of my favorites. It was here that Kerouac was rocketed from literary obscurity into ultimate celebrity, becoming known as the Father of the Beat Generation after the publication of **On the Road**. Thanks to the efforts of Bob Kealing and a handful of Kerouac devotees this particular Florida house of Jack's located at 1418 ½ Clouser Street has become a living tribute, a wonderful writer's residence offering opportunities for a new generation of writers in honor of Jack Kerouac known as The Kerouac Project of Orlando."

—Susan Bennette Lopez

FROM THE EDITOR
Chris Bodor

Congratulations Florida, you now have your own literary journal.

I have spent the last year cultivating this labor of love project. It was rooted from **Florida Speaks**, a Poet Plant Press anthology that "looked at the Sunshine State from every angle." From the success of that book I knew that Florida was worthy of something on-going; something that could be updated issue after issue. The seed was planted and the idea of a literary journal began to blossom.

We ran a contest in April of 2014 (National Poetry Month) asking writers, book fans and poetry lovers to help think of a name. I asked Glenda Bailey-Mershon for some parameters and she advised that the name be "something catchy, one word if possible or else named for some natural feature." She further offered that "It should evoke some strong image." Many clever names poured in. Our favorite, suggested by Mary Rogers-Grantham, was "Coast Lines", but after a few web searches we discovered that the suggested name, as well as many others, were already taken.

The storms began. Brainstorm sessions for a name that was not already taken. Mary Beth, my wife and Poet Plant Press partner, suggested the idea of an acronym. So one Saturday night she and I sat in our Saint Augustine Shores living room trying to combine words to spell out another word. By Sunday night we had it: Ancient City Poets, Authors, Photographers and Artist or A.C. PAPA. Tour guides will recount this story in one form or another when double decker tour buses cruise up and down our street fifty years from now.

With all seriousness, Florida is full of famous addresses. Lanes and drives mark the ground where literary legends walked barefoot in coquina sand and drew inspiration from landscapes of sago palms and palmetto bushes. Jack Kerouac lived in a home on 1418 ½ Clouser Street in College Park at the time **On the Road** made him a national sensation. It was in this home that Kerouac wrote his follow-up, **The Dharma Bums**, during eleven frenetic days and nights. The King of the Beat generation hemorrhaged to death in a Saint Petersburg hospital in 1969. Kerourac was one of many writers who wrote and lived and died in Florida.

Jim Morrison, front man for the band the Doors and a poet in his own right, was born and spent his early childhood in Melbourne, Florida. Morrison did not stay in the Sunshine State for long. The Morrisons were a military family and traveled all over the United States as Jim was growing up. He graduated high school in Alexandria, Virginia, and his siblings were born in New Mexico and California. However, even though it was only for a short time, it can be said that Florida is where it all began for the Lizard King.

Back in 2010 when British singer Billy Bragg headlined the Harvest of Hope Festival in Saint Augustine, an amazing project came across my radar. Previously unheard lyrics written by American folk singer Woody Guthrie, were put to music written and performed by Bragg and the American band Wilco. The fact that Woody never recorded these songs or even added music to them is intriguing. The artistic challenge rested on the shoulders of Billy Bragg to breathe life into the songs the way he thought they should be sung, and Wilco to add the music accompaniments. Since the framework of songs like "Stetson Kennedy" and "Black Wind Blowing" is constructed from Guthrie's unearthed writings, the lyrics are a fascinating window into the sights, and thoughts, and the feelings that moved Woody Guthrie.

I am drawn to Woody's songs from this project that relate to Florida specific themes like Stetson Kennedy and turpentine camps. Located in northern St. Johns County, Florida, the Julington Creek of today is not the same as it was during the times of turpentine camps. Woody Guthrie was a fan of Stetson's 1942 book **Palmetto Country**, and he was invited to visit Stetson at Beluthahatchee, the author's home in Switzerland, Florida. Woody arrived with "five shirts and his guitar" for some "good long talks".

On an easy-to-find Youtube.com video, Stenston himself explains the meaning of this home's colorful name: "a mythical place where all unpleasantness and friction is forgiven and forgotten and harmony reigns supreme."

Another now famous address is the Ernest Hemingway Home and Museum, located at 907 Whitehead Street in Key West. Ernest Hemingway lived and wrote here for more than ten years. There are 52 cats on Hemingway's property. They are all decedents of his 6 toed cat.

It is fun to romance the idea of our writing spaces and stomping grounds being tourist attractions one day. Years from now, will Rich and Amber Cardone's son Theo retell the legend of Tampa's Café Hey? One day in the future, will one of Kimmy Van Kooten's children or grandchildren inform fans of Kimmy's conga infused spoken word days in St. Johns County?

So here you have it—a year's worth of poems, personal essays, and photographs inspired by the Sunshine State, created by the people who know it best.

CONTENTS

My Florida (A Lament)
by Robin McClary

When I was a boy, I could stand on the edge of our town and look out over a carpet of palmettos glistening after a summer shower. I lived in a house whose door was never locked and rode in a car that always had the key in the ignition. Our round TV got one channel. Near our house was a canal where you could drink the water. I have flown airplanes at night where you could fly from one pool of light to another to get to your destination.

These things are gone now, replaced by the honking of car horns, the smell of pizza cooking, the screech of a family arguments and the blasting noise of a thousand TV shows punctuated by a cacophony of electronic beeps and chimes. There are cameras perched on light poles recording our every movement, and the whole state is a vast sea of lights.

I agree that this is an age of miracles, where no child will ever be lost with a GPS on their cellphone and text messaging to their friends. A universe of knowledge lies only a keystroke away. We live in a time where everyone is a public star, and opinions are instantly tabulated. Stores know what you shop for and prices are totaled up as you put the stuff in the cart.

I understand that we have to live in the world that we are given, but I always hold onto those simple moments from long ago. They offer me balance and comfort when the world gets too big and I begin to feel very small.

POETRY

Brian Druggan

Migration
by Mary Deno-Yeck

All day under the blue canopy
       they strip the trees
crimson holly and beautyberry
       staining their beaks and breasts
wind following their wings
       as they beat and beat
the air that calls   erratic
       out of branches
that rise up with them
       relieved of weight.

All day they enter the green umbrella
       sleep silent   intent as thieves
waxwings   robins
       within formations moving them
to each strategic resource
       some pulse
fueling the whole
       of memory's sweep.

I read my history
       on these templates of
evasion   escape.
       They swarm across
my field of vision
       portals to the flight ahead.
The birds concern themselves
       with elements.
I struggle with
       the pulse that names the way

toward what is home
       and what is not.

Adam and Eve in Florida
by Ann Wood Fuller

The evening blinks with lightning bugs and rain.
The fennel softens on its stem
and crowns of cabbage palm and hickory
obscure the milky moon. Humidity,
like glue, confines us to our chairs. We sweat
and rock. The heat: a language that the whippoorwill
repeats, repeats. The garden smells of mold,
and air plants look like demons in the oaks.
The wicker gives and takes and creaks while frogs
ignite their throats tonguing jeweled insects
off the tusks of fronds, and isolated
lamps of houses burn behind their curtained
rooms. In this momentary equipoise,
in air too still to stir, we watch the poison
glisten in the snakes.

Breathe, Mama. Breathe
by Glenda Bailey-Mershon

Mama, let go my hand. Your brain seized.
I'll call Brother. Sister, shake her, make her
breathe—in, out—*Mama, breathe.*

Remember the hurricane, palm trees bowed,
your hands steady on the wheel?
I was six. *Mama, you didn't let go.*

Fever rising. Ice packs, a little ease.
Nurses instruct: pinch her good hand,
rub the blue one. *Breathe, Mama, breathe.*

Visitors come. I stand and watch the flow.
Time slips. I am three. You slap me, break
my heart. *I didn't do it! Mama—let go.*

Three? Three hundred, now. Fingers tease
your burning cheek, heart strung between
groans, pleading, *Breathe, Mama, breathe!*

Relatives come and go. I count memories,
birthdays, anniversaries, seconds. No—
one last gasp, held forever. I breathe,
kiss your cheek. Say *Mama.* Let go.

Florida
by Leny Kaltenekker

When I think of Florida and Saint Augustine,
I think of the most beautiful birds I have ever seen.

They are commonly around,
were water and food abound.

Roseate Spoonbills, Wood Storks, and more,
Terns, Sandpipers, Eagles and Hawks knock at your door.

Ducks, Cormorants, Parakeets they are here.
Large and small Herons, blue or white.
Together with Ibis always look right.
The Pelican dive bombs, catching most fish
which he stores best in his pre-historic chest.

The Egret, however, wins it for me.
My heart jumps a little whenever I see
this elegant creature, so fine, so free.
His black beak and legs with yellow feet
contrast with white feathers, very neat.

All these feathery friends add a luxuriant sight
as they gather in trees and are seen in flight.
This feeling of awe we must not loose
Do not tolerate
cigarette butts and empty bottles of booze
to clutter this land.
Give a hand.
Keep beaches and rivers pristine.
Since we are the stewards of this wonderful scene.

Salt-River Views
by Lance Carden

What was but a touch of pink
        on the horizon
has now turned violent orange
        our seaside-river sky
& its mirrored image
        in the San Sabastian.

The river, moving in obedience
        to the moon,
has again exposed its island gems
        to low-tide decay
        & to the sun,
that even bigger, higher god,
        rising once a day
to put this landscape
        on display.

Nights cast their own
        inspiring spells;
we delight in the stars
        & each new lunar shape.

Even if we're sitting
        in utter dark,
        a street lamp or headlight
        can come glinting
across the waters
        & through
        the head-tall grass,
to settle for a second
        in a long-stem glass.

Beach Glass
by Marie Vernon

Last days I speed the length of shore,
denial hounding at my back.
Gulls etch the sky with vaulting sweeps,
but all the feathers in the world
can no more lift away the loss
than whispers from the sobbing waves.

When lungs and legs can pound no more
I stumble homeward, eyes cast down,
and sometimes glimpse among the wrack
the subtle sheen of sea-honed glass
patinaed slivers caught in spill
of shells and driftwood bleached to white.

Amber, azure, celadon—
pockets filled, I turn to home,
and one more day deny the truth,
while in the house we share apart
a bowl spills full with crystal shards.

Sunglasses
by John De Herrera

Under the Florida sun
Giorgio Armani's are the best:
and when you look up at the late sky
(crossing the state, Alligator Alley
on the Fourth of July)
and see the innumerable plumes,
white whites expanding high
against the azure,
and shades of powder gray
parallel to palm fronds,
jacaranda, cypress, and pine;
the slight, slight rose tint—
it's amazing how much definition
to the brightness they give.

Seeking
by Carolee Bertisch

Along the beach they
take their positions
legs splayed, knees bent
head down, backside up
arms to the sand
hands moving
searching for
shark's teeth.
Man jumps for joy
holds black shark tooth
aloft, smiles broadly,
rides off on bicycle.
Couple kneel at edge
of surf in ocean,
digging a trench deep
in sand to seek.
Striding by, I glimpse
glistening black speck,
bend down to find a
baby shark tooth
perfectly formed.
Then another flashes
in rays of sun, but
when I stretch to
grasp it, shark's tooth
drops from my hand,
disappears through
layers of sand.

Florida
by Ann Kiyonaga-Razon

not a native Floridian
am I

born in Tokyo, Japan
several decades ago
I have since traversed the globe
you could say...

having lived in Central and South America
the subcontinent of India
Europe
and even the Caribbean on a French Isle!
as well as visits to numerous other destinations
some unusual
widespread
in my life I have been made privy to many and various parts
of our gorgeous globe

yet, I have dwelled in Florida the longest
over these many years
it has become our home
our family ventured here some sixteen years ago
children young
we drove into Florida on a beautiful September day
I remember it well as it was our older son's fourth birthday!
stopping for waffles during that September morning, we celebrated
and exclaimed over the palm trees that suddenly seemed so evident
and everywhere
just crossing from the contiguous state of Georgia
to the Sunshine State
it appeared the amperage had risen
sunlight brighter, more luminous...

and Saint Augustine became our destination of choice
we did have plans to peer in on other parts of this elongated state before settling
but this Ancient City touched us
embraced us
Invited us to stay
it was in the very air...

21

not long after our arrival to this area
we ventured downtown
visiting the plaza
taking in the feel of this tourist destination
but I didn't feel like a tourist!
I recall standing by the water near the Bridge of Lions
and there we simply agreed
why don't we just stay here
a monumental decision made with such ease
perhaps because we were simply keeping pace with our destiny...

and this decision
has stood us in good stead
we have flourished here
like the abundant green landscape
thicket of hibiscus
grapefruit, lemon and orange fructification
sweep of ocean and constancy of murmuring waves
salamanders scooting by

interesting...I don't recall needing to adapt
to acclimatize myself to this new place
when we first arrived

always at home here

verdant Florida
gorgeous and vibrant

thank you

Sweet Seraphs
by Gigi Mischele Miller

Sweet Seraphs sing in the heavens
Enrapturing their audience
Bach and Beethoven sit in awe
Vivaldi, Pavarotti, too
Monks chanting free verse in Latin cannot compare
To the sweet singing seraphs, highlights in their hair.

Guardians who watch over us, although we cannot see
Are in our midst among us, ever so faithfully
Sometimes if you listen, near the water's edge
Under a full moon, on a dock or on a bridge
If you close your eyes, for several minutes or more
You are sure to hear the Angels calling from the shores.

Their music will enthrall you, peace and joy you'll feel
Until you tell yourself that this cannot be real, for
Angels cannot be heard by us, you know that's what they say
But surely you will be convinced it cannot be that way
For life without God's Angels, just doesn't seem too fair
Imagine no angels to believe in, I wouldn't dare.

So no matter what the people say, that angels are not here
Don't believe a word they say, for Angels are everywhere!
You can feel them in nature's places, like Guana on the shores
Of the Tolomato River where Timucuan Indians strolled
In wooden canoes, for oysters, in the sunshine of Florida's Jem
Or further south, near the mouth of ancient Matanzas Inlet's rim.

And whimsical Washington Oaks, where a beautiful garden awaits
Take a long stroll, along the paths, just past the coquina gates
Old trees and bugs and flowers and bees, some fiddler crabs, too, you'll see
Snowy Egrets flying by, grand sunsets will lift your spirits, heed!
The beauty of old Florida's relics, the true south, as once it was
And never forget, that in nature, we can feel the angels near us

Outsider
by Robert Waldner

I was an OUTSIDER looking DOWN on your vivid turquoise soul from a highway near the Heavens,
Your waters so clear that I could see your coral heart,

You embraced me with your crystalline warmth while nature sang to me its praises for you,
I listened intently while in the comfort of your cooling breeze,

You held the KEYS to my contentment in my transit to the southernmost,

So I stood there upon my arrival,
Looking OUT into the great blue beyond,
A single steel pole and clarity were the only objects in my line of sight,

I was an INSIDER looking OUT upon your vivid turquoise soul,
My perception so clear that I could see my beating heart

Returning
by Becky Pourchot

At the sea
I am stripped of self,
the contents of my worried cells
released
into the salty sky.

At the sea,
the twisting wind,
the matriarchal waters
call to me,
reminding me
that I am
but a briny creature,
tossed within the waves.

At the sea
my amniotic life returns.
Salt into salt
I am held,
tossed and tumbled
in a
dance of sky, sea, and sand.

At the sea,
the ocean's power degrades my very skin,
making me bare,
it's hungry pulse,
reminding me
that I am nothing but
liquid love,
a primordial being
whose timeless breath
beats within the waves.

At the sea,
I find what I have lost,
my ageless life made clear.
I am born again and again.
Clean, raw, clarity exposed,
with each
and every
pulsing wave.

At the sea
I am a luscious being
brought back the center
of who I truly am
acutely aware of
my fingers
my lips
my heart,
my soul,
alive
only
at the sea.

The Inspired Mic, Beach House Beanery Café, Flagler Beach, Florida

Where Are Palm Trees in Eastern Standard Time?
by Lee Patterson

around now the killing moon
rises about a cornfield's length
over the sea, moths navigate,

long arms reach from trees
where people sit under branches
and hear voices from somewhere

with leaves in the wind
that bites with blue teeth
and brings skin and breath to windows:

perfumed, fragrant spit
words and sliding lips
saying was that you

who said that god didn't live here
not in the moon's light
or above lighted corn fields

that bend in as many shapes
as wind or words can fall
from sliding lips, each good

and whole with sheathed rhythms—
the grass follows
them out of long walks to the water

that says stay here
on the beach to your right side
since no one else can talk to you

not glowing worms in this water,
broken houses with decorative crosses,
or the violet sound of falling anchors—

they name things because they forget them:
people with long fingers
that count the numbers of words

in the lengths of atmosphere,
spaces of the pull of waves

A Place in My Heart
by Bob Patterson

There's a place in my heart where eagles soar free
Where manatee swim beneath tall cypress trees
Where bull gators bellar and wild panthers squall
While giant magnolias shed their blossoms in a fragrant waterfall
Where the noble anhinga silhouettes the wind
Where herons and pelicans glide without end
Where owls screech and otter play
While the smell of jasmine melts the night away

Chorus: My homeland's a place in my heart
               Florida's a place in my heart
               My homelands a place in my heart
               Florida's a place in my heart

Where white ibis drift above high water oaks
While garlands of moss fall like fingers of smoke
Where healing waters babble from unfathomable depths
While schools of fish swim to rhythms of a waltz
Where the sea unrolls its magic and the osprey makes its plunge
Where running sands dance and twirl before the setting of the sun
This exhilaration of wilderness creates a pounding in my heart
Florida's a place in my heart

Chorus: My homeland's a place in my heart
               Florida's a place in my heart
               My homelands a place in my heart
               Florida's a place in my heart

A Bed on the Ocean
by Nancy Bevilaqua

awaken to offer
or suggestion of a wisdom kiss
whisper flood   sand is washed   although

they're stranded sea things gesture that their vision
is still whole

mammoth of night tide switches over
before dawn   how soon we've come together
as before   hot there too and cauldron

safer blood between us now so yes a kiss to eat
the best of me   hold it out for all to see

bowl of clouds surrounds us
reach down   fish will gather at edges
of your flesh   ask your mercy one last life

gulls ignore us barely diving   ship offshore
cargo for the sky to burn

spell gone soft out there   they fish
for days   scar the currents
with a finish of the pliant scales

crustaceans stranded or they've come to shore
to bury life   to keep it going

that's the cave   Atlantis drowns as you
are sleeping   orange and peach   infinite
morning   Venus is engrossed in me

vibrations of spirit shapes   they spool by on the beach
step my path for just a little sun   at home

we quiet   would lick the skin around each other's
thighs   hold moons between our bellies in my furtive
fertile mind

A Rough-Edged Cracker
by Dotty Loop

I'm a Florida cracker,
    Also Redneck through and through.
I wear K-Mart flip-flops,
    And my trailer has a view.

Y'all might think I'm country,
    and possibly you're right.
I just enjoy my comforts…
    Life shouldn't be a fight.

I drive a rusty Nissan
    with all my hub caps gone.
But just so it's enjoyable,
    Who cares what car you own?

Life's a box of chocolates,
    The fun is in the choosing.
Sit there in your Cadillac,
    I'm out there stock-car cruising.

And when life is over,
    Look back at what you've done.
Nothing matters any more
    But did you have some fun

Floating on Rough Water
by Lynn Skapyak Harlin

Jacksonville July
heat brings storms
gray day overcast, hot breeze.
No job, no money, kids at her ex.
Waiting for change,
seeking some solace.
She needs to move, for a spell
feel worry free.
Mickler's Landing, water churns, chops.
White caps rush to shore, slap the sand.
She is riding the waves,
keeping herself up, head high
chin out. Big toe pointing at dark sky.
Smile lights her face as water swirls,
churls, twists, whacks, turns her around.
There is calmness in the tumult.
Floating on rough water,
her life now, not always, just now.

Rhiannon Lee

Kayaking
by Jane Lynahan Karklin

The kayak meanders through Sarasota mangroves
those areas of subtle darkness
dappled here and there with rays of sun
to dance across the water, shining
with reflecting tiny stars.

The kayak skims the water
oars dip and rise, dip and rise
propelling you onward.
The soft wind kisses your hair
giving you the sensation of flight.

Cormorants and pelicans observe you
then return to their avian lives,
their inner world, their outer beauty
their perfection.

You watch it all from your kayak
the fish are jumpin'
and Gershwin's "Summertime" wafts across the water
mixing with the sun and the echoes of nature
becoming life itself – your life
the one you were meant to live
not the hectic life you're living now.

Turn from that world of constant noise and anxiety
welcome yourself into this serenity of sky, of water
because you are this nature
you are this world
you do belong.

–First published in **Adrift Within Dreams** (2012)

Go Away Fall
by Kimmy Van Kooten

"Go Away Fall!"

Let me climb into your limbs and lie in your crook where I'll stay warm
Let me embrace all the leavings of yesterday and keep you from any harm
I'll sprawl out on your bark
I'll go deaf to the wind
I'll go up against anything that tries to rip you apart, and gladly keep your bright colors alive and
tell of the summers we've spent
together, forever!

Go away, Fall!

The Turtle
by Tonn Pastore

The turtle is like me.
Awkward slow on land
graceful in the water
I am graceful in environs
if liquid
I get stuck in sand
lose my balance
especially on one leg.

It loves the water
must return to the beach
to keep its love going
to pass on the purpose
to love its better parts.

Its hard protective shell
a shield that rejects
slings and arrows
mortar shells lobbed
from the fray.
A side impervious to the world.

When upended
off balance unable to trudge
to the happy destiny
waiting for me in the water.
The underside vulnerable
to the darts thrown my way.

It needs a helping hand
when on the beach.
Leaving behind the fragile
best parts of them
buried in a shallow place.
Barrier needing to be around
those parts to keep the danger
away long enough for the
loving parts to grow.

The turtle is like me.
It is grateful for the help.
It is in love with the beach.
That is where the heart
he loves is walking
along the edge of his liquid
floating universe.

Marie Groves

Joyland
by Stevie Cenko

She rides past Joyland, the country-music dance hall
that used to be her Momma's barn. She peers through
the window to see the dance floor where bales of hay
used to lay and Dwayne first kissed her.

Rain rolls off her Cracker cowgirl hat, onto her poncho.
Tied around her neck, is the faded, blue bandanna
that once belonged to her Pa.
The gator she wrestled years ago became the boots
she still wears to protect her from the snakes.

She sold The Double D Ranch. It's now downtown.
She gallops into Pruitt's Drug Store on her horse, Silver,
the wheelchair, with her bullwhip and service doggie
to rustle up some killers
of pain.

A poem about an older, Florida Cracker cowgirl,
as she rides through the downtown that once was her family's grand ranch.

Seduced By the Moon (Again)
by Kathleen Roberts

I am seduced by the moon again–
Larger than life, a ball of white light
Hanging onto the edge of the earth;
Begging me to come to her–
Shimmering thru the branches
Of the sycamore tree,
Repeating patterns on the porch boards.
I bathe in my nakedness before her,
The energy moves thru me
As I shimmy–
My belly dancing motions like waves
In her shadow.
I move, like leaves on the trees
Sister moon nods her approval–
Whole in my pureness
I am free to be me!
We are one.

Florida
by Nadia Ramoutar

My adopted mother
You took me in as a wayward child
Orphaned by a reluctant mother
New York may have
That statue of the woman
But you nurture and embrace us
The new immigrants
Seeking beauty and eternal light
Beyond merely fictitious roads paved with gold
You are richer than famed parks
Your treasured jewels linger
In endless sunrises and sunsets
Spewing fuchsia, crimson, gold, bleeding over rapid or passive
Mystical healing Waters where tides churn fiercely
Invading soft taupe sands or rivers peacefully meander
Between ancient hanging trees
Blessed am I
To be your beloved Child
Though I have not always been so grateful
Mourning my birth mother
You patiently waited
Giving me Freedom to roam
To come and to go, ebb and flow
Celebrating my homecoming
Without question nurturing me
The perfect mother
Loving unconditionally
Expecting nothing in return.

Florida's Environmental Heritage
by Beverly A. Bell Kessler

The beauty of this ancient land
Threatened by man's interference,
Can be brought back to what was intended
By Florida's amazing endurance.

We restore the farmland now barren
From poisonous pesticides,
Above contaminated waters
Where wetlands once resided.

Our pledge to the lost ecology
Of birds, fish and small prey,
Is to bring forth what was destroyed
By man's unconscious trade.

Our human population
Has increased our water's demand,
Which in turn has limited nesting
And endangered this beautiful land.

Every species supports each other
Yet, we see them shrink away.
So, we maintain habitats for animals
Mitigating where man went astray.

Everything has a balance
It is how we all survive,
Yet, some kill for other reasons
Than just to stay alive.

Those with deep convictions
Have come to serve the need,
And watch their contributions
Grow forests from a seed.

For the panthers, fox and deer,
And Florida's birds of ancient times,
We'll sustain and balance our heritage
By the consciousness of Mankind.

Sunset Passing Near Bushnell, Florida
by Ginna Wilkerson

Faded yellow canoe belly with scuffed paint.
Her child-like legs crossed and propped,
burlap of scratchy summer grass beneath
tender back skin in a thin cotton shirt.

Me, driving down I-75 at a determined 80,
catching a glimpse of scruffy saffron metal–
imprint of memory in long-ago connection:
a slender hand flopping into the marsh.

Acres and miles of marshland and hammock,
dozens and hundreds of high-school boys
bestowing dearly-bought Wal-Mart jewelry.
She stands, stretching gracefully, now out of sight.

I drive on south, fading egg-shell tinted sky
announcing sunset – a corner of the car revels
in pink-edged merlot haze, reeling in the day
like a plump-striped bass in August twilight.

Back there, she walks up the path, tucking away
a stray wisp of pale hair. In my mind, teen-aged
melancholy suits her, closing the day's door
with a little dance around her tiny bedroom.

Old Lady at the Flea Market
by Alan Catlin

They must come here
every week whether they
need to or not, these old
ladies in wheelchairs, with
walkers, canes, surgical
stockings stretched over
swollen ankles, varicose
veins as they creep down
the aisles, stopping traffic
both to & fro, harder to
get around than The Seven
Rocks of Granite, blue hair
permanently waved & frozen
into place by aromatic sprays,
house dresses reeking of
mothballs & sweat, as they
go on talking, oblivious to
all else, occasionally eyeing
the goods laid out on tables,
pausing only to rearrange,
their handbags wrapped nine
times around their wrists,
you might have to amputate
to remove one against their
will; they touch stuff but
they never, ever buy.

My Maggie
by Lee Weaver

1964, my Maggie marched with protestors
One of many whites walking with the coloreds.
An exciting time of resolution and dedication for her.
For me, a time of separation.
When she was off demonstrating I hung out with my buddies.
I wouldn't march with her.

My Maggie was a Yankee girl from Chicago.
I was from right here in Saint Augustine.
The South.
Middle name Stuart, Last name Lee
I wanted to believe I was kin to Jeb and Robert E.

She made me
Take my stars and bars off my rear view mirror
And scrape the decals off my side windows.

Small price to pay
To be with my Maggie
The prettiest gal in Saint Augustine.
She loved me and I loved her, My Maggie.

When she came back from D.C.
She talked about King

Dr. King this, Dr. King that.
I kept quiet.

She'd drink out of the colored folks' drinking fountains.
White folks would say things to her.
She'd just smile and say, "I have a dream."
Her words would rile them even more.

I said, "you have dream fever."
She'd smile and say, "Yes, I do. Yes, I do
I have dream fever."

She went to Atlanta one week
To protest, to march, to demonstrate.
One night, while she was gone
I went to the middle of town with my buddies.

We'd heard this Young fella, Andrew Young, was coming
From Washington D. C.
To our town, my town
Saint Augustine
To lead a demonstration.
He came with two hundred marchers to the plaza.
Young told them to wait on the corner
While he came over to talk with us whites.
Many were Klansmen.
I was there.
I was with them.
He had guts, coming by himself.
Soon's he got near
We jumped him.
One of my friends got him on the head with a lead zap.
Down he went.
He got up
This Andrew Young
Stubborn colored man here in my town.
Clipped on the chin, down he went again.
Got himself kicked in the belly, kicked in the back.
I kicked him in the head.

He got up again
Stubborn, tough colored man
Here in my town.

Cop made us stop.
Told us to let him say his piece.
We did.
He did.
He had guts.

We followed him as he walked back to his marchers
This Andrew Young
This stubborn colored man.
I watched him disappear into his crowd.
And there she was

My Maggie.
My Maggie had seen it all.
She'd seen me kick Andrew Young in the head.
Our eyes met.
She looked broken.
I knew I'd done the breaking.
I looked down.

When I looked up, she was gone.
She knew what I was.
I knew it, too.
A racist.
I never saw my Maggie again.

Foot Soldiers Monument, Saint Augustine, Florida

Grey Hotel, New Berlin
by Tim Gilmore

In just that way the wood was weak but certain,
soft from age but brittle carapace,
I knew when I first set down my bags
that I'd long known this place.

Its porches fit me, and its warped halls,
that strange off-center bedroom
with its lonely sideways attic window,
that century without electricity.

The place remembered my being here
like my body remembered how to swim
in the cold lake after long sickness,
and my body felt the place remember.

That jigsaw porch bracket fell into my hand.
My foot stepped through that second-floor slat.
Candles and chimes in the wind from the river
determined the night in the lightless rot.

I found that rot so comfortable.
The hotel felt like childhood at night.
I came from the river. The building was boarded shut.
I slept well there for a week, a stray dog on my feet.

The Grey Hotel in New Berlin, just north of Jacksonville, was built sometime between 1870 and 1880. It barely lasted to make the Jacksonville Historical Society's "Most Endangered Buildings" list in 2007, after which it was demolished.

HAIKU

Daniel Florez

The Haiku Mind
by Michael Henry Lee

Exactly what is the haiku mind? I dare say I'm not sure. In upcoming issues I hope to explore a few of the components, that when successfully comingled, may produce a state of creative and philosophical awareness conducive to writing the genre of poetry known as haiku.

In this our inaugural edition I will attempt to provide a brief history and definition of a perpetually misunderstood art form.

The roots of haiku begin around 700 A.D. and reflected a rigid 5-7-5-7-7 syllable count and was referred to as tanka or choka form. As with any art form transformations occurred. Tanka morphed into linked verse or renga and by the mid-16th century poetry had been embraced by the peasant class; becoming less rigid and came to be known as haikai and later renku. It was not until the 17th century that the father of what is considered modern haiku; Basho, would popularize hokku poetry which later came to be known as haiku.

For the last 400 years the debate over what is and what isn't haiku has continued. Most grade school children in this country have had some exposure to haiku, and most likely one of their first adventures in creative writing was in producing a three line poem comprised of 5-7-5 English language syllables. The teacher dutifully presented his or her very rudimentary 40 year old plus definition and for a lot of us that was it. My introduction to haiku started just this way and sparked a fifty plus year creative love affair. It was not until within the last decade that my understanding of haiku was, shall we say enlightened to the novice level I'm enjoying today.

English language haiku is a poem one to three lines in length, comprised of seventeen or less English language syllables, that generally follows a short long short cadence The poem has a seasonal or nature reference (kigo) most often appearing in the first or last line of the poem. Finally haiku poems appear as two parts not as one long description or narrative. There is a break between the kigo and the rest of the poem; two entities that compliment or expand the meaning of the other no matter how subtlety.

Here is arguably the most basic definition of modern English language Haiku that I can hope to offer, and do any justice to a highly venerated art form, philosophy, life style, even to a way of thinking, the haiku mind.

Michael Henry Lee is a haiku and senryu poet who moved to Saint Augustine in 2004 from south California. He attended the University of Missouri at Kansas City, receiving a B.A. in Sociology with a double minor in Theatre and English. He is internationally published. His work has appeared in Frogpond, Heron's Nest, Mainichi Daily News, One Hundred Gourds, and Haiku News, among others. Michael received an honorable mention from the Mildred Kanterman Memorial Merit Book Award for his collection of poems **Against the Grain** (Eleven Hour Press, 2013).

endless summer
the wind in the palms
on a postcard

Vilano Beach
the call of shark's teeth
from beneath the pier

Summer Haven
the morning noon and night
of rain

Antoinette (Toni) Libro is a member of the Coquina Haiku Circle and the Haiku Society of America. Her haiku, tanka, haibun, and other poetry have been published in a wide array of journals, including Modern Haiku, Frogpond, Moonbathing, and Red Lights. Her haiku will appear in the Haiku Calendar for 2015 as the result of a contest sponsored by Snapshot Press (UK). She and her husband reside in Saint Augustine, by way of New Jersey, following her recent retirement from Rowan University.

river winds –
on the "no fishing sign"
belted King Fisher

Paula Moore has been seriously writing haiku for the past four years. She is a founding member of the Coquina Haiku Circle of N.E. Florida and her work has appeared in: Modern Haiku, Frogpond, a fine line, Chrysanthemum, Haiku News, and Contemporary Haibun Online. Paula is a graduate of UNF in Jacksonville with a bachelor's in Language Literature. After a three decade career in HR Management Paula took an early retirement to dedicate her time to; writing, gardening, travel, and enjoying her grand kids.

cicada song…
a warm breeze twists
the hanging moss

EXAMINING FLORIDA:
A CLOSER LOOK

ESSAYS AND ARTICLES

Brian Druggan

Eartha White and Ottis Toole: Good and Evil in Jacksonville
by Tim Gilmore

I wanted to write about Eartha White, "Jacksonville's Angel of Mercy," before I wrote about pseudo-serial-killer Ottis Toole, Jacksonville's "Devil's Child."

I'm embarrassed to say I first imagined one book about them both. *Eartha and Ottis* or *Ottis and Eartha* would be a big decentralized narrative in which the two of them represented the polarities of good and evil on the stage of their North Florida city. Luckily I realized the idea was terrible, not to mention a crime against Eartha White.

So **Stalking Ottis Toole: A Southern Gothic** appeared in August of 2013. The book is disgusting and I'm embarrassed I wrote it. The story is important and I'm proud to have written it. It plays all the different versions of Ottis Toole against each other. His IQ was said to be 75 and he confessed to every horrible crime police put before him like a little boy trying to get as much attention as he could. The book is as much about story and what people do with story as it is about Ottis Toole.

Nevertheless, I feel corrupted by **Stalking Ottis Toole**, and I've looked to Eartha White to cleanse me. How selfish of me! Hopefully it's at least less insensitive than putting them together in one big Southern-Gothic Urban-Omnibus of Good and Evil.

Eartha White founded the Clara White Mission, which she named after her adoptive former-slave mother, and in which she lived for almost 40 years until she died at 97 in 1974. Today the Mission is the best-known humanitarian institution in Jacksonville, though the important black neighborhood of LaVilla has nearly disappeared from around it. In a time when black citizens were at best ignored, Eartha started a nursing home, an orphanage, an adoption agency, an employment agency, and homeless services that served black and white people alike.

Though seven or eight books had made mention of Ottis Toole, and almost as many had been promised or planned, no one had published a book about Toole before.

Nor has anyone published a book about Eartha White, and that's far more surprising. Her story forms a chapter in several books, like former Congressman Charles Bennett's 1989 **Twelve on the River St. Johns**.

Bennett came close to naming the wealthy white man Eartha believed to be her father, but in a footnote, he echoed an 1890s' army pension investigator's judgment that it was "not necessary to ventilate an old affair" by saying that since publishing the name "may intrude on the privacy of living persons, that information is not included here."

Historian Dan Schafer truncated his manuscript on Eartha shortly after he began it in 1976. Before he helped house Eartha's papers and materials in the University of North Florida library, he worked through them in the back of Eartha's cottage at Moncrief Springs. Sometimes when he came north of Jacksonville to Moncrief, he'd find that people had broken in and burnt Eartha's effects in metal barrels to keep themselves warm.

Schafer is as gracious a person as he is eminent a historian. He shares his knowledge and his thoughts with me as I sit across a coffee table from him in the high-ceilinged and wide-open living room of the bed-and-breakfast he runs with his wife in Jacksonville's old Riverside Avondale district.

But my project is not his project.

Though racism persists, times are different than they were in 1976. If I were a young white man writing about Eartha two years after she died, I can't imagine I'd presume I had the necessary sensitivity.

A local newspaper article from 1982, six years after Schafer started his manuscript, still said he was writing Eartha's biography. The article names Eartha's biological mother, but calls her biological father "a prominent white man," perhaps the first mention of that combustible open secret in print.

Do I have the sensitivity and understanding now? I'm not writing an academic history. Clearly there's no way a middle-class white man in 2014 could understand what it was like to be Eartha White. How much more despicable then was my *Eartha and Ottis* conception?

In 1968, the poet Nikki Giovanni wrote:

and I really hope no white person ever has cause
to write about me
because they never understand
Black love is Black wealth and they'll
probably talk about my hard childhood
and never understand that
all the while I was quite happy

I'm not so much a white man writing about Eartha White as I am a lost man writing about his search. It's of that I continuously remind myself. Though I won't ever understand what it meant to be Eartha, I want to come as close to the true Eartha as I can. At least I'll give her story new life. Maybe I'll influence someone else to do better.

And is it equally selfish of me to hope this city's "Angel of Mercy" wouldn't mind offering me the chance to do what little good I can by writing about her? If writing about Ottis Toole poisoned me, I hope it doesn't sound too fatuous to say that I hope Eartha White might save me, even if she died five months before I was born.

A Poet's Fear
by Becky Meyer Pourchot

My hands trembled so much that the words on the paper seemed to do a little jig on the page. I hoped the audience wouldn't notice or in the least would be sympathetic to my nervous state. This was big. I wasn't just casually reading to a crowd, I was in a competition, a charity event that I had devoted months of my life to assemble.

"I'm not nervous," I told myself and my friends, not just in the moments before, but in the three weeks prior when I practiced my poems out loud to my bedroom walls. There were no shaking hands as I spoke to my empty room, but now with one hundred eyes on me my nerves were untamable.

War of the Words was an event organized by myself and my two friends, author Tim Baker and organizer Nadine King as a fund raiser for Nadine's charity, Christmas Come True. The plan was this: to pit four authors, poets, story tellers up against each other in an event that blended prize fighting with the open mic tradition. In an added twist the audience chose the winner, their votes acting as raffle tickets.

Standing on stage, I told myself I was more excited than scared, but my body argued otherwise. My hands were so wet with sweat they stuck to the paper. My stomach spun in loops in my belly. Ignoring the panic in my body I took a deep breath and started out my poem slowly:

> At the café
> I see you,
> a king settled in his throne,
> your eyes crinkled
> in a glistening gleam
> and I wonder what you think
> when my gaze lands upon you,
> taking in the lure of your heat bright sun…

I looked around at the audience and could feel their breath, slowed and attentive. They were with me, unaware of the slam dance my heart was doing in my rib cage. I decided rather than fight the fear I went with it and channeled my energy into the poem:

> …And I want…
> I want to reach out my hand across the table
> feel the articulated bristles
> that spring from your jaw.
> My hand cupped on your chin
> I want to bring my mouth in to your cheek
> so I can
> taste the heat on your skin.

Though I denied wanting to win, somewhere in me I really wanted to. So I spoke outward, to the crowd, from the pit of my stomach, pouring out not just the feelings in the poem, but releasing all of the tension I held inside.

I smile and nod
as you speak words that
build your
swagger and conceit…
and hopelessly
I am weakened,
smitten by your arrogant charm
But instead I sit…
and listen
with reserve,
trying to think of nothing,
but dullness and cliché,
And I want…
I want….
…oh fuck it!
I am climbing this table,
knocking glasses,
plates and silverware aside
and as I perch,
like a happy raven
I lean in close
my face up to yours
and
I will kiss your lips,
without subtlety
without reserve
without doubt,
letting the hunger of this inner beast
dine on her desire
And in this moment
my heart, my hands, my lips
will speak to you
And finally
you will know
exactly
what
I want.

My muscles released with my final words and I felt the tension slide off of me. As I stepped off that stage I was no longer concerned about what the audience thought, but instead just savored the glowing warmth of completion.

To my disappointment I was knocked out in that round and a subsequent round. Though not what I had hoped, the success of the event made up for it. War of the Words raised $1600 to provide Christmas gifts, trees and dinners for families in need.

As writers sometimes we're thrown out of our comfort zone. It could be trying a new genre, learning to market a book, writing a press release, or in my case organizing an event and reading poetry to a large group.

For writers, and all humans, when we force ourselves into new territory there are inevitable challenges. I think of it like swimming in a foreign ocean, with a mystery of creatures beneath you. You're never sure what you'll run into. But when we try new things, in the midst of the fears there is growth, pushing us to be something greater than we are.

As a person who is used to sitting behind her computer organizing words, performing my poetry on stage was scary, but now I understand more about myself as a writer. I'm just a wee bit bolder and braver, and no longer so afraid of the fear.

Florida: The Write Place
by Larry Baker

The land of this story was one square mile of Florida real estate halfway between Jacksonville and St. Augustine. A mile of beachfront and a mile deep into the scrubby interior, cut along the eastern edge by Highway A1A as it went south toward the Keys. - **The Flamingo Rising**.

I live in Iowa, but I seem to write about Florida. Four of my five novels are set there, especially in and around Saint Augustine. I get asked "Why?" all the time.

I've always had a quick answer, "I used to live there." But, truth is, the reason is more a matter of chance than choice. And it might not have happened that way unless I saw a particular stretch of coastline along A1A back in 1988.

Long before I moved to St. Augustine in 1988, I had managed movie theatres in Texas and Oklahoma. In the late Sixties, I had managed the Admiral Twin Drive-In in Tulsa, Oklahoma, and the Winchester Drive-In in Oklahoma City.

The Admiral was one of the biggest drive-ins in the world. A lot of weird stuff happened to me in those days: my July 4th fireworks almost setting an adjacent funeral home on fire, finding a dead woman sitting on the theatre toilet, selling sex education books car to car, and more. All in all, fodder for fiction, but I was not a writer yet. I had the material, but that was all. For years I had been telling my students about those days in the movie business, polishing the stories, both remembering and inventing details. When it came time to actually start writing a novel, my theatre days were the obvious first choice for a subject.

That first draft? It was incoherent. Worse, it was boring. I was missing two things: a unique locale for the story, and an interesting narrator. The narrator question was solved after my wife and I adopted two babies, both gorgeous, and both from Korea. As I re-thought my theatre story, I realized that the story was not really about the crazy manager. It was about being raised by two tilted Southern parents who raised their kids inside the screen tower of the world's biggest drive-in theatre.

I wanted a story that was larger than life itself. What better than a story about the world's biggest movie theatre? And where to put that theatre? Apologies to Oklahoma, but a larger than life story needed a larger than life location; or, at least, a location that would seem totally incongruous for a drive-in theatre.

Florida was waiting for me.

My wife and I packed up our two children, loaded a van, and moved to Saint Augustine in 1988. For the first year I lived there, however, I worked in Jacksonville. Three days a week, I drove up A1A to the University of North Florida. Anybody who has driven that route will recognize the spot I passed all that time...that atypical curve in an otherwise straight A1A. It's full of condos now, but back then it was empty and undeveloped. And I had a vision, which I turned into the vision of Hubert T. Lee, fictional owner of the fictional Flamingo Drive-In, as described by his son Abraham in **Flamingo Rising**:

> *"This is the spot for my Great White Wall," he had told my mother, pointing to a large half-moon-shaped indentation that pushed A1A in a long arcing curve away from the ocean. Another visionary might have seen a perfect spot for a tourist hotel fronting a hard beach that could accommodate pale and flabby easterners and their two-ton cars. My father saw a drive-in theatre.*

And that decision...to place my fictional drive-in on *that* plot of land...that is the "chance" I mentioned earlier. As soon as I visualized the geography of one piece of my story, the rest of the Florida references became not only automatic, but necessary.

With hindsight, however, I can see how Florida is the perfect locale for most of my stories, especially in and around Saint Augustine. As I continued to write **Flamingo**, I realized I could add specific details, each with a literal meaning, and those would eventually become symbolic. Two in particular became especially important: the ocean, and the fact that Saint Augustine is America's oldest city. The ocean is life and death.... note which characters in Flamingo do *not* get in the water, and what happens to them. And as a symbol of human pride, that giant screen tower sitting on the beach facing the ocean, that plot of land on A1A was perfect. The narrator of the book is Abraham Lee, and his mother explained to him how his father described the Tower to a reporter from *Life* magazine:

> *When he told the young man that he had built this Tower to be his home, to be indestructible, to withstand the mightiest hurricane, to protect his family from the wrath and pettiness of almighty God... well, your father was not teasing at all.*

Florida supplies the best weather and the best ocean. Saint Augustine is itself a perfect symbol for history. And the histories of my human characters' individual lives are themselves set in a city with the most history in America. My appreciation of the universal theme of history is most evident in my favorite Florida novel, **A Good Man.**

A story also requires people more than places, and Florida provided a few of those for my books too. First, a caveat. You must understand the difference between a character being *inspired* by a real person and a character being *modeled* after a real person. Except for myself, as a somewhat deranged theatre manager, none of my characters represent real people. A young woman in St. Augustine had certain traits that I used in a character in a short story published in 1994. As I was finishing **Flamingo** in 1995, a New York agent, who had read the short story, called me and asked if I had a novel with that character in it. He would want to read it and perhaps represent if it was any good. I was on page 144 of **Flamingo** ... the character was not in the book ... I immediately told the agent, "Yessir, I am working on a novel right now with her as a main character." And thus was born Alice Kite. I was writing a scene that was introducing a different character, the nymphet Polly Jackson, and I added the character from the earlier short story to that scene, and the entire book changed. A lot of people in Saint Augustine think they know Alice Kite, but she does not really exist. She is compelling and mysterious, but she is not real. She is fiction.

Flamingo did introduce another major character for me, the only one who is both inspired by and modeled after a real person in St. Augustine, and I even use his real name: Fred Tymeson. I met Fred in a classroom at St. Johns Community College. I was his history teacher. He was older than me. He was a St. Johns County fireman. He was a handsome Vietnam vet, and the coeds were smitten. In **Flamingo**, I had to create a Giant Fire at the end, foreshadowed in the first lines of the book:

My name is Abraham Isaac Lee, and I am my father's son. This is a story about Land and Love and a Great Fire that consumed all my father's dreams.

When it came time to write the scene, I needed for some local firemen to show up. Why not Fred? The narrator remembers how he first met Fred the Fireman a few minutes before the fire begins:

A handsome fireman named Fred Tymeson, his name printed in large letters on the front of his uniform, had a private conference with my father. I could see the two men speak slowly, and then Fred patted my father gently on his back, as if to console him.

I did not realize at the time that Fred and I would become close friends over time, and he has been in almost every book I have written.

Flamingo Rising was my first, and it is most readers' favorite of all my books, but I see it as practice for my subsequent books. I see a lot of writing flaws in it, technical stuff about points of view and chronology confusion, problems that I was more aware in my following books. But it does what none of my other books have ever done...it makes you cry at the end.

My second novel, **Athens/America**, is the only non-Florida book I have written. It was clearly based on my political experience in Iowa City, where I live now, and where I served two terms on the City Council. **Athens** has been described as a "cult classic" by one bookstore. I think that means nobody ever heard of it and the only copies still in existence are in a box in my basement. But its publication did insure the end of my political career.

Athens, however, helped me understand my strongest creative urge, something I had been doing in my first two novels without even realizing it. Other writers, I am sure, have confronted these same issues, but for me the sudden clarity of the questions was itself a revelation.

What is the line between fact and fiction? Can real people inhabit the same world as fictional characters? How does a writer use reality in fiction to produce truth? How much of reality is itself fiction?

And thus was born my favorite Florida novel, my favorite of all my books: **A Good Man.** Not only would I use real people in fiction, I would make a real town...Saint Augustine...fictional. Not only would I use words, I would use pictures too. **A Good Man** is full of pictures of Saint Augustine, but placed always in the context of where that real location is being inhabited by fictional *and* real people.

The cover art is a picture of my son and I from almost thirty years ago on a Saint Augustine beach, but that image becomes a memory for the main character, Harry Forster Ducharme. Open the book and the first photo you see is that of the Bridge of Lions. A few pages later, you will see a picture of Harry's Curb Mart, where Harry Ducharme cashes in a winning lottery ticket in chapter two:

> *. . . he finally found his store. Painted across the front and top width of the building were the most profound words he had read in ages: Through These Doors Walk the Finest People on Earth "OUR CUSTOMERS." Harry walked in and became a finer person. The Curb Mart was a convenience store out of the Fifties...the southern Fifties. Hanging over the front counter was a rack of camouflage hunting suits for toddlers, complete with lace across the top. Behind the counter was a locked cabinet of assorted ammunition. Chewing tobacco and snuff were stacked neatly, and he could even see a butcher shop in the back.*

And if I was back in Saint Augustine, why not bring in characters I had created for my first Saint Augustine story. But that story ended in 1968. **A Good Man** begins in 2000 as Harry wakes up:

> *Knee-deep in the Atlantic, squinting east toward a red dot on the horizon, Harry Ducharme was trying to remember the first line of a story......As his mind cleared, he slowly remembered driving past a high-walled fort, across a bridge guarded by lions, past a lighthouse, past a liquor store, parking his Buick...well, that was still a bit fuzzy, where he parked it.*

Now, bear with me here as I almost get too philosophical, but as I wrote **A Good Man** I explicitly understood that the existence of **Flamingo Rising** was itself a fact, and I would use the characters of that story in a completely new story, but it had to be somehow consistent with the past fiction. You still with me? **A Good Man** is thus two Saint Augustine stories at the same time: the new world of Harry Ducharme overlaps with the old world of Abraham Isaac Lee, Alice Kite, and Polly Jackson ... each of them now 32 years older.

Harry Ducharme walks into Harry's Curb Mart and meets a grown-up Polly Jackson. Harry is hungry and asks Polly for a recommendation. Where does Larry Baker like to eat when he is in Saint Augustine? At the Manatee Café. So, obviously that is where Polly sends Harry, but not to the location of the Manatee now, but where it was in 2000. As Polly says, standing at the cash register of a real and a fictional Harry's Curb Mart:

> *"All you need to do is turn left out of the lot here, go a mile or so until you cross the railroad tracks, straight through the light and you'll dead-end on San Marco, turn right and go past the D&B school until you see a carousel on your right. The Manatee is directly across the street, but parking is a mess, so start looking early."*

> *Harry thanked her and was about to leave when she called after him, "You get there, you tell Cheryl that Polly Jackson expects a free breakfast for sending her a new customer. You do that, okay?"*

The real Cheryl from the real Manatee Cafe is now in the same world as the fictional Harry Ducharme and the fictional Polly Jackson. But I think she was pleased with Harry's reaction to her food:

Harry got to The Manatee in a few minutes. He soon found himself seated in the best organic and vegetarian café in the world, drinking a just-brewed cup of coffee. After eating his eggs and potatoes, watching the café quickly fill up, and sipping on his second cup of coffee, he admitted that Polly knew what she was talking about.

Over and over again, as I wrote **A Good Man**, I had the pleasure of re-experiencing the sights and sounds of Saint Augustine, but through the perspective of my fictional characters.

His gypsy days were over, and he would need a permanent home soon enough, but for his first day in St. Augustine Harry was still a tourist. He parked downtown across from the Cathedral and walked for hours. He had seen it all before, old towns that lived off their history. St. Augustine had more than most, but there were still the gaudy and borderline-tacky gift shops up and down St. George Street, the carriage rides along the bayfront, the locals in period costumes. But the core was genuine. It was a damn pretty town, he had to admit. Robber Baron hotels converted to colleges and office buildings, Tiffany stained glass windows everywhere, bouncy blond coeds, tanned the old fashioned way, but no longer a temptation for Harry, who surprised himself by still possessing a smidgen of self-respect. But, of course, he soon found a new favorite bar tucked between touristy shops on St. George Street. A small overhead sign with the key word: Tavern. Noon, time for lunch, Harry walked into the dark narrow tavern and sat at the bar. He was surrounded by a dozen people, and none of them looked like tourists. In their own way, they looked like him.

I used to live near Magnolia Street, and I wanted Harry to experience the pleasure of my memories of that street when he went looking for a job:

Magnolia Avenue was aptly named, its aged trees arching from each side of the street to meet overhead, forming a leafy green ceiling. Sunlight filtered through, but the street was still a shady forest, and Harry found himself walking slower and looking up more and more. Years earlier, National Geographic had named Magnolia one of the ten most beautiful streets in America. The "Things to See in St. Augustine" pamphlet put out by the tourist bureau always cited the magazine's endorsement, and made Magnolia a must-see destination for out-of-towners. Unprepared, however, Harry felt like he was the first person to have seen it.

The above passages are deceptive, seeming only to describe a real street or tavern, but they are good examples of how the physical environment of Saint Augustine is necessary for me to convey the themes of the story itself.

Harry is a lost soul, a literal orphan who was pulled out of an Iowa river sixty years earlier and adopted by Quakers, washed up on the beach in Saint Augustine on Election Day-2000, stepping on the shore of America's Oldest City, his own history serving as a burden to carry, hungry in body and spirit, finding food, but also finding temptation as he steps into the St. George Tavern. Harry is a functioning alcoholic. But even after he swears off liquor, he is still at "home" in the Tavern. Indeed, most novels are about history...how else to explain an individual's "present" except by knowing his history. Saint Augustine is Harry's last chance, and **A Good Man** is the story of his redemption.

Florida is a southern state, with all the history that goes with being Southern: land, race, rebellion, defeat, and northern occupation. But Florida is also more polymorphous than the other southern states in all those same areas. Snow Birds, Crackers, and a catalog of hyphenated Americans...Cuban, African, Haitian...political conservatives, and social liberals careening off each other, a lot more Florida novels are waiting to be written.

The Fermented Apple *(A love story)*
by Lou Graves

The voice (or rather style) of any artist (be they a writer, a painter, a musician etc.) is realized only when (and if) the artist finds themselves faced with a hermetic world; a place in which to bury themselves and become lost within its quintessence; a world which they can claim as theirs and theirs alone. Woody Allen's New York, for example (with its uptown trysts and taxi cabs, with its braless Annie Hall, and its absurdities and neuroses, and adolescent memories of Brooklyn) is a different city altogether from the New York of Lou Reed (with its transvestites and neon lights, and its Coney Island high school sweethearts) Likewise the seedy and austere Los Angeles of Charles Bukowski is a far cry from the brooding, melancholic Los Angeles of Jackson Browne. Paul Simon, Truman Capote, Frank O'Hara, Martin Scorsese, Patti Smith, Sir Arthur Conan Doyle, Irvine Welsh (the list just goes on and on) all created, through their art, an hermetic world informed by the city in which they lived.

Saint Augustine, unlike New York, is a small and sleepy city (a drinking town with a fishing problem perhaps) however like New York, and like any other city, she is haunted by history, by the countless untold stories forgotten like bottles of wine in dark corners gathering dust. The ghosts that haunt Saint Augustine, unlike those of New York or New Orleans, are quiet spirits, content to lean on walls or read newspapers, or to walk down cobblestoned streets whistling or tossing coins in the air; they are in no hurry to get anywhere and can make a second (or two) last as long as five or six (or even seven) would in any other city. She is a city where the distance between dreams and reality vanishes and the line separating them is both vague and shifting, intangibly tangible and tangibly intangible. She is that glorious moment of drunkenness where anything seems possible, where the sky is at your feet and you feel capable of kissing the stars and the moon (and the man on it) She is a city haunted by a strange kind of timelessness, an hermetic loneliness if you will. If New York is the city that never sleeps, then Saint Augustine would be the city that never wakes up. If New York is the big apple, Saint Augustine would be the fermented apple.

My Saint Augustine therefore, the hermetic world defined by my art (my art being informed by the city in which I live) is unique only to myself, just as somebody else's is unique only to them; the subjective truths of my world and the subjective truths of theirs are bound together only by the objective truth of our Ancient City and are distinguished by their countless nuances and idiosyncrasies which happen only when we allow this objective truth (the city in which we live) to inform our art. My Saint Augustine is a hard drinking woman with golden sandy hair and ruby lips (lips that curse like a sailor) and her voice is the haunting echo of an echo of a distant melody at midnight while at her feet lay the ashes of eternity and a shadow cast by a sun which is setting. She is often tired. She is often sleepy. But always she is dreaming.

In composing the preceding paragraphs I was reminded of one slow afternoon when the sun was buried in the rainclouds and small puddles of rain littered the streets like dirty mirrors. I sat in the darkest corner of a dark bar with a pint and a packet of cigarettes. Meg was behind the bar pouring a glass of wine with the radio on low as the distant sound of thunder rolled across the sky and echoed (and echoed). The bar was empty save for a couple sitting at a table nearby talking quietly. I took out my notebook and began to scribble some unintentionally senseless and enigmatic lines (I was struggling with the last stanza of a poem) Slowly the lines became nothing more than words, words that soon enough became nothing more than spilled ink, senseless inkblots. I set the pen down and began to listen (to the thunder, to the radio, to the sound of Meg's footsteps on the hard wooden floor) and began to eavesdrop (the worst of the writer's bad habits) on the couple sitting at the table nearby. They were talking about things they used to do as children.

"I used to climb trees" he said "and pretend I was sitting in the clouds looking down on everything and everyone. I used to pretend I was some kind of god"

"I used to lie on the grass" she said "and stare up at the clouds daydreaming and try to see what I could see in them, what kinds of shapes I could find in the clouds"

I looked down then at the marble bar (as mercurial and as clouds undulating on a stormy day) and began to compose (first in my mind, then in my notebook) a one act play about an old drunk, down on his luck, staring into a marble bar and reminiscing on his childhood.

Another time (as I sat in the same bar, in the same dark corner) I was told by a half-drunk girl in a green dress that Saint Augustine was "the city that never wakes up" I wrote this down in my notebook thinking about how I could use it (in a poem? in a short story?) and began to string together images that would describe Saint Augustine as I saw her, as a hard drinking woman with golden sandy hair and ruby lips and a voice haunted by the echo of an echo (of an echo) of a distant melody at midnight with the ashes of eternity at her feet and a setting sun casting her shadow. *She is often tired*, I wrote, *and she is often sleepy. But always she is dreaming.* I set the pen down and finished my drink then, ordering another Guinness, I began to look around the room watching as the city, with all her echoes and shadows, all her untold stories, all of her nuances and idiosyncrasies, passed slowly by. And I was tired. And I was sleepy. And I began, staring into my Guinness and getting lost in its mercurial haze like rising smoke, I began to daydream.

Fakahatchee Bay Crossing
by Jim Draper

December 8, 2010 Ten miles west of Everglades City, Florida

"Damn, are we going to have to paddle across that?" Words oozed around the ambergris lodged in my throat.

"No option. We can't go back." Andy held on to the trunk of a mangrove. One of about a dozen that rose out of an oyster bed on the edge of Fakahatchee Bay. He fished the charts out of his day pouch. The wind and waves were beating our kayaks together and us into the trees. "We need to skirt up." He squared his compass on the charts.

"Skirt up?" *Christ. I am going to die.* Day four of a seven day jaunt through the Ten Thousand Islands. Looking into the churning water yet to cross, this day would be my last.
We broke camp early that morning and shoved off from White Horse Key. The plan had been to snake our way through the mangrove islands and pitch tents on Dismal Key. Stay there for the night and then head out toward Jewell Key the next morning. A loop around Dismal rendered less than ten square feet of dry ground. No campsite anywhere.

Midafternoon found us tracking toward Fakahatchee Island, a big land mass with a historic shell mound on it. A lot of high ground. Camping there for the night was our only viable option.

Andy dropped his compass back into his pouch and folded the charts. He held his paddle to his nose and sighted due south. "That is where we need to be." The blade pointed across the torrents toward a speck on the horizon.

"You are shitting me." My grip tightened on the mangrove. "I can barely see it."
"Nothing's going in our favor. Tide's pushing us in to the east. Wind is blowing us west." Andy worked his kayak skirt over his head. "We need to go south." He nodded into the tempest.

"That's the only high ground there is." I reached behind my seat and fingered a rolled up piece of fabric. My skirt. Never had put it on.

This was not the best time for trying something new.

I secured my paddle and wedged myself up into the mangroves tight. The black skirt went up in the air. One arm went through the opening and then the other. Once it was over my head I pulled it down and snapped the elastic strap around the cockpit. *Dang. I can't believe this thing fits.* The bilge pump foot snuggled past my waist and hit the floor between my thighs. I pumped it a couple of times to prime. Muddy water sloshed out.

I looked up. "Andy, I really don't know if I can do this."

Andy laughed. "Well, what's your plan?" He nodded over his shoulder toward the low December sun. "It'll be dark soon. You can sit here all night and whine about it or paddle to the other side."

Andy snapped his gloves into place and pointed his paddle to the far point on the horizon. "That's where I'll be."

"So how do we do this?"

"Head out perpendicular to the waves. You can handle your boat better going at a right angle into the peaks than riding the troughs. Loaded like we are the up and down would kill us."

"But that's not the direction we're going."

"You'll see. That's gonna keep you steady. The wind will shove us sideways."

"You sure?" Andy was twenty five years my junior but he knew these waters well.
"No fucking clue. But that's what I'm gonna do." He laughed. "We'll get to land one way or the other." He took his blade and pushed out into the bay. " We'll know when we get there if we did the right thing."

"I'm not sure that's funny."

"Probably not." Andy paddled hard. "Follow me."

Years prior I became bored with religion and made a deal with God. *I won't offer you suggestions about how to rule the universe and you don't tell me how to think.* At the time it seemed like a good deal for both of us. God and I went our separate ways and neither of us suffered from the break up. *Well old guy, I guess we have reached that inevitable point.* My path looked like lentil soup on a rolling boil. *You can't call up a buddy you haven't talked to in years to get him to help you out of a jam. I get what I deserve.*

I let go of the last twig of hope, shimmied myself into deep water, dropped my rudder and locked my left toe down hard on the port footbrace. *I guess I'm right. What in the hell am I doing here. Why did I think that this was a good idea? You fucking idiot, you are way too old to do this shit. Your mid-life crisis should have been over ten years ago.* I beat the waves with my paddle. My kayak sliced dead on into one wave after the other, each time I was completely under. Each slack second I could grab I gripped my paddle hard with one hand and pumped the bilge pump with the other. The water that sloshed in the cockpit was soiled with the piss and puss that fear wicked from my kidneys.

Twenty yards out, thirty, forty. Each wave crashed into my bow. *You ain't. Beat me yet.* I cursed Neptune's wake.

"You alright?" Between swells and splashes Andy's red kayak would show.
"Alright." *Not really. I am going to die. I know it.*

A half hour in. Fakahatchee bay. Hard straight wind from the east. White caps and rough was all that could be seen to the west. The sliver of mangrove island where we had skirted up was showing faint. The distant high ground of Fakahatchee Island inched above the water. "Jim. My hatch is leaking." Andy voice bounced over the waves. "I'm taking on water. Going to high tail it straight down the troughs and try to get to land."

I could see his freeboard had gone. "Go for it." He was swamped. "OK, buddy, you're on your own." Andy's paddles churned. "See ya on the other side." *Damn.* "OK." *So this is the way it ends?*

There was a peace. Bobbing like a cork in the middle of a saltwater bay. To the east a couple of miles of churning water then an endless labyrinth of muck and mangroves. To the west, more churning water with a few hundred oyster beds topped with a tangle of the short trees then the Gulf of Mexico. *Fuck it. Dead one way or the other.* I plunged my paddle down hard and made a ninety degree turn. My bow lined up with due south and the destination. Fakahatchee Island popped its head up above the waves.

My body found a rhythm. I rode down into a trough. I corrected to the left and floated to the crest. I paddled like Hell. Right left pull pull. All my pain went away. Strength came from a place I didn't know I had. My kayak plowed through the water.

The fact that the water in Fakahatchee Bay is shallow should be reassuring. Being over six feet, I could probably touch bottom pretty much anywhere in sight. The problem is that under the water is a bottomless sea of mud. The few solid masses are beds full of razor sharp oysters. Tipping and standing up was not an option. If I were in the water the sloshing would rip me to shreds over the shells.

Mangroves ran up port. I could see that the water broke out calm ahead. Andy was sitting still pumping his bilge like crazy. His freeboard was growing.

The water smoothed. I tucked my paddle under my arm. The pump sucked gallon after gallon of brine from its place in my groin. *We made it.*

"Well, that was fun." Andy grinned as I paddled up next to him. Leeward of a mangrove island gave us some protection.

"Yeah it was." *It was. Thank God.*

To the north I could barely see the point we had held onto those last mangroves. I looked down at my hands, my paddle. *Dang. Survived.*

Or did I? Maybe I died out there. I looked toward the middle of the bay and that place that inspired a hard right turn. Somebody died. A scared, insecure, whiny bastard who didn't want to let go of the last mangrove died in the middle of Fakahatchee Bay. He drowned and was sliced to pieces by the oysters. The crabs shred him to bits and were passing him up the food chain. The person who got to the other side was someone else. I had to figure out who that was.

"Let's set up camp." Andy tapped his paddle on the bow of my kayak.

"Yeah, where we headed tomorrow?"

"We'll see, we will see."

Scene in Florida: Photo Essay
by Charlie Cawley

I am an artist who uses a camera to produce images as fine art. The world I live in makes the art and I get to capture it. I have been engaged in this process for some 30+ years now.

You should know that I fall in love with the visual delights that I can capture with the camera and share with others. During this time I've had the opportunity to live in different areas of the country, those being: Southern California, New Mexico, Central Florida (St Petersburg), North Carolina, and now St. Augustine, Florida. Hopefully this will move toward that "scary" proposition of retirement. "Scary" because I have no idea what to do when I retire. Photograph and write I hope.

Through all that time I've been an engineer, a photography teacher, a photography lecturer, and have written a book with photographs about my experience as a photographer and my love for the medium.

I don't ever like to play the game of judging that any one of the areas I've lived in is more photogenic than another. The visual world is there or wherever I go with my camera. The photographer Garry Winogrand once said "I am a tourist everywhere I go." I agree with him. I get to move about in this life with much the same attitude. So of course my times living in Florida have most certainly included many scenes I've recorded during those times I lovingly call "taking my camera for a walk." The images in this essay are appearances captured during my times in Florida.

In a philosophical sense photography is first and foremost about light. We get our small time frame on this Earth immersed in the light. I believe my time is about recording the light, drawn to it like a moth circling the light bulb or the plant pushing its gorgeous flowering to the sky. It is a very inherent and ubiquitous driving quality of all life. The light is of course here in Florida so I'm off to capture it, with its humor and grace and all, so I can share it with you. Because THAT is what is most important for me.

Scene in Jacksonville

Charlie Cawley

Scene in Orlando

Charlie Cawley

Scene in Saint Augustine

Charlie Cawley

Charlie Cawley

Charlie Cawley

FOUND IN FLORIDA:

A PEEK
AT UNIQUE LOCATIONS

Brian Druggan

Embracing the Loneliness: Jack Kerouac in Florida
by Susan Bennett Lopez

I was born in Rockledge, Florida at Wuestoff Hospital the same year as the last Apollo flight, the Apollo-Soyuz Test Project; it was a time of American discovery and not long after Jack Kerouac had died of internal bleeding brought on by alcoholism in St. Petersburg, Florida. My father was a Dust Bowl Oklahoma farm boy turned Engineer at NASA and as such we did our fair share of travelling and moving as he continued with his aerospace work.

Years later, as an adult I moved back to Florida for the fifth time in my life. Heavily dependent on library card catalogs and community college literary collections I found myself deeply entrenched in my Kerouac studies. I only had an Internet connection for a few months, using a growling dial up AOL modem and a snail slow, muddy beige no-name tower computer. I spent my nights trolling Beat Generation sites and often got lost in thought on Levi Asher's Lit Kicks page, the best online Beat reference of the early Internet era.

I lived on a quiet cobblestone street in Winter Park, Florida lined with a gothic canopy of Southern Oak trees dripping with Spanish moss, the sound of bats and lovelorn bull frogs clicking and chirping at one another 24 hours a day.

Tacked to my kitchen wall for inspiration were quotes I'd gleaned from my Internet searches about Jack Kerouac, this from Dharma Bums written during one of Jack's handful of Florida stays, "I saw that my life was a vast glowing empty page and I could do anything I wanted." I was surrounded by post cards and pictures of Jack, Allen Ginsberg and William S. Burroughs every morning as I drank pots of coffee and twitched out poetry on my 1950's olive green manual typewriter. I often looked out my window with immense wonder, peering at a giant magical Oak, surrounded by a mass of ferns in the center of my yard, wondering if this was THE tree in the photo of Jack in Florida standing with hand on hip, long sleeved striped shirt open over white t-shirt, peering somberly off the page yet still endlessly handsome.

It was during this same time that journalist Bob Kealing, discovered the history of Jack's time in Orlando, setting in motion the push to create something bigger, and it all began with the publication of Kealing's article for the Orlando Sentinel. Jack had in fact lived nearby; as it turned out he lived in Florida several times in the late 1950's and 60's. I felt such a synchronistic connection with Jack that I wanted to believe THE tree was behind MY home though I knew in all probability that it was not. If I had only read Kealing's article when it was published, the mystery of the great oak tree would have been revealed, ultimately inspiring me to keep moving forwards with my own literary adventure taking the short fifteen minute drive to Jack's place from my own tiny back porch apartment.

During the late 1950's Jack Kerouac lived just northwest of downtown Orlando, on a quiet street in a College Park neighborhood, not much different from mine. He spent many a humid Florida night toiling away until dawn working on his book "The Dharma Bums," one of my favorites. It was here that Kerouac was rocketed from literary obscurity into ultimate celebrity, becoming known as the Father of the Beat Generation after the publication of "On the Road." Thanks to the efforts of Bob Kealing and a handful of Kerouac devotees this particular

Florida house of Jack's located at 1418 ½ Clouser Street has become a living tribute, a wonderful writer's residence offering opportunities for a new generation of writers in honor of Jack Kerouac known as The Kerouac Project of Orlando.

Each day as I drove to work, the dots of my own Kerouac journey continued to connect, I unwittingly travelled over the Sanlando Springs stretch of I-4 towards Altamonte Springs where Jack had once envisioned a dream home for his sister and her family, his mother and himself. The land Kerouac once owned, now underneath a portion of interstate paving over his dreams, a small stretch flowing into the concrete veins running throughout the state.

In that same year after calling every name among Jack's friends whom I could track down from reference books, I discovered the Jack Kerouac School of Disembodied Poetics in Boulder, Colorado. I found myself on the phone with a quite generous and ultimately forthcoming writing lab assistant who gave me the home phone number of the prolific poet and controversial writer of "Howl," Allen Ginsberg.

In all my youthful naïveté I was on a journey to ask every question and turn every stone until I got to the core of Kerouac's psyche. It was too late for me to ever know Jack, but at that age I felt all the pieces were there and only needed to be put in place for me to understand him.

With my heightened literary aspirations, sitting at my managerial job in the back office of the Orlando Italian Oven Restaurant, I took a deep breath, swallowed my fear and dialed Allen Ginsberg's number. Bob Rosenthal, Allen's long time personal assistant answered the phone several long rings later.

The words that spilled from my mouth in a jumbled blur were greeted initially with a quite curt response as Rosenthal pointed out, "young lady, until you can ask questions of Mr. Ginsberg that have not already been asked a thousand times, I suggest you continue consulting your books, you'll find your answers there." Crestfallen at how close I was and feeling the moment slipping away from me I did what any hungry young Beat scholar would.

I asked Bob Rosenthal to start over. "I think we got off on the wrong foot, I've been listening to "Holy Soul Jellyroll" in my car all month. I even made a sculpture of Mr. Ginsberg inspired by a photo of him from the earlier days. I'd love for him to have it."

Rosenthal took a deep breath and I could feel the protective tension melt away. "You said you were calling from Florida?" Awash in enthusiasm and nodding into the phone I answered "mmm hmmm, Orlando."

He continued, "if you are anywhere near Sarasota, Allen will be performing at the Sarasota Opera House and doing a book signing next week I can put you on the list and set a ticket aside for you if you'd like." It was that moment that molded the shape my Beat Generation research was to take, pulling me on course with history and allowing me to almost touch the past.

A skinny young twenty-something boy wearing a too small silver sequined shirt stood in front of me talking to Allen, as he flirted Allen glowed beatifically. When my turn came, my vision tunneled and my entire body quaked, I handed him the sculpture encased in a small shadow box frame.

Allen Ginsberg looked at me sternly through his horn rimmed glasses, mouth pursed, peach fuzz wisps of hair along the dome of his wise head. The seersucker jacket he wore over a deep burgundy shirt hung squarely from his large shoulders along his thin frame. My confidence was wavering as he chuckled, a tender smile overtaking his face, warm brown eyes softening.

"I had a lot more hair back then! How about a picture?" he said pointing to the sculpture and gesturing for me to take a spot at his side.

The exchange may have been brief, but Allen Ginsberg changed the way I saw myself as a woman, no matter how that may sound, he did. I crouched by his side trembling in my skin when he abruptly turned, speaking to me, inches from my face. His bold poet voice boomed as he instructed, "Stand Up. Woman! Never stoop for ANY man." He paused, "BE BOLD. You have in your grasp the makings of greatness!"

The metaphor of "standing up" not lost on me; I confidently took my place at his side, waist length hair cascading down the stripes of my shirt. I stood, absorbing the words of advice imparted upon me by one of the most influential writers of his generation.

I smiled, I could not stop smiling. I embodied that smile and that moment and embraced his genuineness.

"Will I see you tonight at the Opera house?" he asked as I was turning to go. I nodded and slinked away dumbstruck by the encounter.

Following his performance, I had the welcome opportunity to speak with Allen again. He signed a sketch I did of him on the stage along with my ticket. Without pretense, I talked briefly about my journey towards knowing Jack Kerouac and how inspired and moved I was by Allen's bravado, I felt I knew so much of Allen's story in trying to get to the heart of Jack's. I was cast into the stars standing in the cobblestone courtyard outside the opera house speaking candidly with him.

It was that night in Sarasota that Allen Ginsberg encouraged me to go to St. Petersburg, Florida, "start at the end and you will find your beginning" he wisely advised.

On a day trek, across the state East Coast to Gulf Coast, I drove. My beat up gray Volkswagen Fox, a five speed with a broken reverse carried me on my pilgrimage towards Jack's final home.

Mix tape blasting the Dream Warriors on my low end VW cassette deck, "I've lost my ignorance and don't know where to find it so I searched furiously" as a humid wave of salty air blasted through my cracked windows, each moment closer to Jack. With nothing but my tattered old Rand McNally Road Atlas and a general sense of direction I continued on my quest.

St. Petersburg was a grid of one way streets leading to neighborhoods full of one story cinderblock homes, tiny run down ranch houses with crab grass lawns and chipping paint. In St. Pete, no matter where you were you were only a few streets from the water. You could smell it in the air, and as such there were a lot of beach hobos and otherwise nefarious types. I drove the streets in search of Tenth. I stopped with windows rolled down to ask directions with little to no luck.

After a few hours of roaming I encountered a scraggly old bearded man, eyes a bit wild, hair a yellowy white, he wore frayed denim shorts and a dingy dirt tinged white Panama Jack t-shirt, the picture of a faded blue and red parrot curled around his hunched back as he weeded around a tangle of elephant ears in a poorly kept flower bed near the cracked walkway of a tiny lot on Tenth Street.

He limped over to my car, the stale smell of layered sweat and ocean salt wafting from his leathery pores, an orange tint on his nicotine stained facial hair encircling a mouth almost devoid of teeth. He leaned uncomfortably far into my open car window, flecks of sand stuck in his bleached arm hair crinkled against the dark interior vinyl of my car. I asked him about Jack.

"Got Five Bucks?" he blurted, I fumbled through the change and found a few crinkled bills in the cup holder. As he reached for the money he pointed a crooked finger down the block, "You missed yerr man by about 20 years or so girl…but it's on down that way on the corner."

Exhilarated and a little scared, I wanted to get on with it. This guy was not the kind of man I would typically ask for directions or intentionally roll my window down and invite into a conversation. He asked for a Camel Wide Cigarette, gesturing towards the pack my brother had left on my messy passenger seat. I thanked him and gave him the entire pack of smokes, quickly putting the car in gear; it lurched forwards causing him to withdraw from the window. I may have been recklessly youthful but I certainly wasn't stupid and knew when it was time to go.

In the mid-nineties most cameras still took Polaroid pictures or film, cell phones weren't commonplace and social media did not exist. Life was about encounters, experiences, opportunities taken and moments that you dare not allow to pass by. It wasn't about pictures. Procrastination was deadly to experience so I lived my life in every moment creating my own story often detailing the memories in my journals for looking back on later.

It was enough, for me to stand outside the home I knew Jack had once occupied. (Assuming the scraggly man had steered me right.) The humidity so languorous, wrapping around me like a thick muggy sheet of air, about as welcome as the cold beads of sweat running along my ribcage.

I knelt down and touched a crack along the sidewalk, picturing lonely Jack, sad alcohol swollen face, staggering home with a bottle in his meaty, strong working man hands—quietly cursing to himself as it slipped from his fingers and broke the tiny stretch of earth below. I imagined Memere stirring a pot just inside the house…a small veil of steam softening her face, cloaking her features as she shifted her weight impatiently waiting for Jack's return.

I wondered how many nights he had shuffled across this very ground, laying under the stars on the scratchy crabgrass lawn, looking up into the vast blackness worrying about Sputnik.

In that moment, it was in the experience, and for me THAT was enough.

I felt closer to Jack, his loneliness was palpable, I FELT the breath of his words in the soft arid breeze – I relished the literary closeness I had longed so deeply for.

A month later I found out that Allen Ginsberg had died. Deeply devastated, I was humbled by my encounter with him and thankful for his wisdom and the opportunities he encouraged in me, thankful to have met him in person and lived in that moment – closer to Jack. Thinking of Allen as I sat on Kerouac's crumbling pavement walkway I smiled, I could not stop smiling.

1418 ½ Clouser Street, College Park, Florida

Backstreets: A Creative Sanctuary in the Nation's Oldest City
by Robert Waldner

Today, Spanish Street looks a little different than it did at the beginning of the millennium. Looking north from Treasury Street you can see two gaping holes in the landscape. The hole on the east side of the street once held an establishment that, for the better part of a decade contributed a great deal to the local arts scene in Saint Augustine, Florida. From 1999-2006, 61 Spanish Street had a name that didn't sound much different than those of many other cafés or coffee shops. However, when you walked up onto the patio and in through the front door you could instantly sense what set Backstreets Coffeehouse apart from all the rest. It held the essence of individual expression free from the common stereotypes that obscure the world's beauty and give the misguided illusion of conformity.

There was the intermingled scent of incense, strong coffee, and cigarettes. It was the perfect fuel for artists creating their next big piece. Custom wallpaper still adorned the interior of the building from its days as a "Castles of The World" museum. The gothic theme of the walls was complimented by enigmatic original art, much of which was produced by the many eclectic patrons of Backstreets. Overhead floated ceiling tiles customized by individual artists with pictures, poems, and tributes to the Nirvana that they had found during their late night endeavors around the Ancient City. Over the house speakers of the establishment always played a variation of soulful songs meant to soothe the mind and massage the heart into a state of inspiration.

By day, Backstreets was a haven for those who wanted to break free from the bustling world outside. It was an environment conducive to sparking the embers of free thought. By night, it was where the day's artistic renderings were displayed for locals and tourists alike as musicians and poets shared the inner workings of their souls.

My personal experience with Backstreets started in October of 1999 when I met a coworker there for coffee before work. Having only lived in Saint Augustine for three months I was employed at a downtown retail store only two doors away from the new coffee shop. Being a twenty-year old New England transplant with a passion for writing poetry and a healthy admiration for all forms of art, I was looking for a place in town to embed myself like a shell in the coquina walls of the Castillo. I found that place the moment I crossed the threshold into Backstreets and embed myself was what I did.

I first met Dawn Quackenbush when she took our orders that morning. My coworker and I sat in two very comfortable, orange, 70's style bucket chairs at the rear of the building. Dawn approached us with an ear to ear smile and a comforting voice which displayed not only a genuine happiness that we were there but also a deep pride in her spirited place of business. She and her boyfriend Jarrod Lapato had opened the doors less than a month prior to my first visit. With Backstreets, they had created a centerpiece for a small, intimate city rich in history and immersed in individuality.

Backstreets did what many places could not for the local working youth in Saint Augustine. It gave them a place to go after their daily grind where they could be as important as any tourist to walk through a local business's front door. This was not a beachside café with fruity cocktails and Jimmy Buffett playing over the house speakers. These walls contained no awkward, forced conversations over candlelight. This was a destination enveloped in creation. The building exhaled inspiration, which we in turn inhaled and recycled into art.

Kat Vellos remembers her days of patronage at Backstreets fondly. Like many others who entered the front door of 61 Spanish, she was an artist and she circulated her passion and vision both through and upon Backstreets and its clientele. Kat had a passion for poetry and wanted Backstreets to be a place where people could come together and share their creativity, insights, fears, loves, imaginations, and inspirations. That is when she founded Poetspeak, a twice-monthly gathering where poets displayed their hearts and souls for all who were inclined to listen. Before starting Poetspeak, Kat was travelling to Jacksonville to attend poetry readings. She saw the potential in Backstreets to provide a haven for poets right here in Saint Augustine. So, in the early months of 2002, she pitched her idea to Dawn and Jarrod, which they accepted with open arms.

Kat was a student at Flagler College from 1996-2000. As it was for many other students in town, Backstreets was a place for her to grab a coffee in the morning or in between classes as well as a place to let loose at the end of a long day spent in Flagler's graphic design studio. Immediately upon Poetspeak's inception, the literary open mic gained a following of poets and enthusiastic listeners alike. At each event Kat would see anywhere between 20-40 participants from as far north as St. Marys, Georgia, Jacksonville, and all over the first coast. "There was a small group of regulars who showed up each time, but there were always at least one or two new faces in the crowd," said Vellos.

Those being the days before social media, Kat along with some of her friends would print and post flyers all around Saint Augustine and Jacksonville to get the word out about Poetspeak. She also placed ads in FolioWeekly and the Gargoyle, the student newspaper for Flagler College. Once the event gained popularity, one of the two monthly gatherings included a special appearance by a featured poet– on these nights Poetspeak's attendance would swell to 50-75 attendees. A two-dollar donation was requested at the door as a way to compensate the Featured Poets, and to cover printing costs for promotional flyers. Kat remained the curator and host of Poetspeak from its beginning in 2002 until 2005 when she moved from Saint Augustine to Seattle. Poetspeak eventually faded away, but not before it had made a big impact on the community and planted the seed for another poetic outlet in town, the Ancient City Poets.

When I asked Kat Vellos about her time with Poetspeak and how it has impacted her life she answered simply but insightfully, "I think about it all the time. Poetspeak has been one of the things I've done in my life that I'm proudest of. I would never have met the wonderful people I've known if I had never made it happen."

Musically, Backstreets was in the direct path of the abundant young talent that flowed through the alleyways and red brick streets of the Ancient City. It was right in the middle of the historic district, yet slightly west of the heavily tourist travelled paths of St. George Street and the Saint Augustine Bay front. It gave performers the option to play for a younger local audience in a more intimate setting.

There was a plethora of unique musical talent on any given night. Some performers were just passing through town. Others had become house favorites that drew a growing crowd with each show in the small intimate space of the coffeehouse. Bands like Whisper 2000 with their alternative rock ballad style and "3" whose acoustic rage was accented by the unique depth of the didgeridoo gave the Backstreets faithful a variety of music genres to keep them coming back. Well- known local solo musicians like Amy Hendrickson and Sam Pacetti carried the Ancient City ambience and tugged at the heart strings of the audience with their deeply personal lyrics and stellar guitar playing. With the sale of beer and wine, Backstreets became a popular hangout for the young locals.

One of the biggest bands to leave their mark was a young group of First Coast natives who called themselves Tribolotomee. The band's core members were Marshall Pyle (AKA Granpappy) on vocals and guitar, his brother Chris Pyle on drums, and Robby Armstrong who was the bands bassist but also made contributions on guitar, vocals, and percussion. Through the years Tribolotomee welcomed many other artists to their roster of band members, including Melvyn Nurse and Owen Aschoff on percussion, Eric Nicolino on guitar, keyboard, and backing vocals, Tim Moffitt on saxophone and clarinet, and bass guitarists Dan Brown and Tai Welch. Tribolotomee's original introspective lyrics and tight instrumental cohesion always drew a crowd that seemed to push the physical boundaries of Backstreets and make it look as though the building was about to bust at the seams. The band members were not only performers but also hometown guys who would stop in regularly for a coffee, a beer, or just a good conversation.

Recently I had the chance to reconnect with Granpappy. I asked him to reflect on his time as a young Northeast Florida musician, Tribolotomee, and their days of playing at Backstreets. In his reflection Granpappy stated, "Backstreets represented a declining presence for youth in Saint Augustine. When I was in high school in the early '90's at Douglas Anderson in Jacksonville, we had Einstein a Go Go, an all age music club. It was the epitome of a forever-growing scene. I was a part of the Fenwicks band. We played Admiral Spicoli's, a Saint Augustine club located just over the Bridge of Lions on Anastasia Island. Other great bands came through there. Whorlman comes to mind.

"Flash forward to Backstreets in the late '90's. I had moved away and come back. Jarrod and Dawn made a home for poets, artists, and musicians. Creative juices stained the walls. I love these memories, so much diversity. Backstreets defined the scene musically right there. It was different. It was not Reggae Sunday. It was not boring."

Granpappy moved out of state in the early 2000's and now lives in Asheville, N.C. where he continues to grow as an artist, musician, and an individual. "All of the members of Tribolotomee still thrive and make music, together sometimes, but all solo too. Chris Pyle is wrapping up his first studio session where he is on guitar and vocals. I (Marshall) have a self-produced two volume EP slated to be released. Robby Armstrong has continued to record his solo music as well, which both my brother and I have contributed to," stated Granpappy in regards to the current status of the founding band members.

Backstreets was not your run of the mill coffee shop. It served a bigger purpose than to turn out coffee to the waking construction workers and business professionals in town. Sure, they made coffee (really good coffee), but it wasn't meant for mass production. Nothing about Backstreets was mainstream or manufactured for the overall population. There was a soul there that started with a vision shared by two very passionate people.

"Cheers is probably where it started for me," said Jarrod in a recollection of what inspired him to open Backstreets. "I always wanted to have a place where everybody knows your name. I dreamed about it as a teenager. Then I went to FSU for business and finance and met Dawn. I graduated college a year before her. When she graduated we went on a 17-day backpack adventure through Europe, staying in hostels or sleeping on the train. One of those days, after dumping our packs in the lockers at the train station, we set off to explore the city. We eventually found ourselves in a really laid back coffeehouse somewhere out and about on the streets of Amsterdam. We ordered a few pints of Heineken and settled into the couch for hours. It was during our time in that coffeehouse, drinking beers, listening to The Doors, talking with some of the locals, and just "enjoying the local flavor" that I turned to Dawn and said, "We could do this!! Let's open a coffeehouse when we get home." She never really took me seriously, but in the back of my mind I knew we had to do it. After moving to West Palm for a while and looking for jobs to no avail, we eventually moved in with my mom on Vilano and found jobs in Jacksonville. Dawn took a teaching job and I was in a management program at a finance company. The summer after our first year in Jax we began the search for a coffeehouse location."

As it turns out, distancing Backstreets from the main tourist focal points was part of the business plan. Whereas most businesses in Saint Augustine aim to cater to those who flock to the area for the beaches and history, Dawn and Jarrod wanted to capture the charm of the Ancient City but also play a role behind the scenes.

"We knew from the start that we wanted to cater to the locals and not be a part of the St. George Street tourist circus. We had very limited start-up funds and a shoestring budget. 61 Spanish Street fell right into both of those categories, but it needed a lot of work before it could function as a coffeehouse. It was only one block away from the main tourist strip and right where many of the locals passed by each day on their way to their jobs, which, by the way, is where the name Backstreets came from. It was a simple reflection of where we were located.

"So, we spent a few months reconfiguring the interior, installing a kitchen, building the bar, etc… We started gathering a few pieces of furniture, all of which we found along the side of the road. It was pretty pitiful, actually, when we opened. I think we had two tables with four chairs each in the front part of the building and maybe two couches and a chair or two in the back "lounge" area, and the four-seat bar. I think we did about thirty dollars in business the first day, but we knew once word got out, those who "got it" would love it. Just the same, those who didn't get it would hate it. We had plenty of both.

"One funny tidbit we always look back on and laugh at is, after all the work we did for months on end to get the place ready, the day before we opened we realized neither of us knew how to make a cappuccino or even what the difference was between that and a latte. We were clueless!! We got some instructions online and thought we had it figured out. Within the first few days, one of our first regulars kindly asked us what the hell we were doing to his espresso drinks. He set us straight and explained how we could make it better. The rest is history."

History is what Saint Augustine is all about. There is an ambience and an aura here that is unmatched almost anywhere in the United States. Dawn and Jarrod came in with the understanding that this town had a presence far beyond the pastel colors, fruity flavors, and high priced theme parks that are most commonly associated with Florida. They "got" that the Saint Augustine locals had a passion for art, literature, and music. They provided a place to display what the Ancient City is all about.

Backstreets is now just a very vivid, very fond memory for many people who came to know and love it. Dawn and Jarrod eventually came to a place in their lives where they had to move on from the early mornings and late nights of providing to the local flare. The building was demolished in September of 2013. The life of Backstreets was relatively short for a business in such a historic city. It was open for seven years. It was not a family business handed down from generation to generation. However, it served a very important purpose, to provide a creative sanctuary for those who needed it most. It added an important page to a very long history book.

I have fond memories of Backstreets Coffeehouse. It was one of the first things I experienced as a young person on his own after moving a long way from home. One of those customized ceiling tiles was mine. It hung directly over the bar where I sat many nights, submerged in inspiration and at times oblivion.

I personally have a very special friendship with Dawn Quackenbush and Jarrod Lapato. I recently had the chance to reconnect with them after nearly a decade. They met my children for the first time. We watched fireworks on the Fourth of July from the Fountain of Youth. When I was young, they provided a place for me to grow as a writer and a person. They strengthened my connection with the Ancient City. I owe so much to them. Their names, along with the business they so proudly operated should be written in the Saint Augustine history books with permanent ink to be remembered by all who breathed the inspiration imparted by Backstreets Coffeehouse.

MOMENT IN THE SUN:
WRITER SPOTLIGHT

PRIS CAMPBELL

LeeAnn Kendall

Florida, to me, is a stir-fry of different cultures, landscapes, age groups, snow birds and the glorious sea surrounding it all, sizzling under the hot Florida sun. Go north far enough in the state and the South edges over the border; west, more cities reflecting an older, more relaxed Florida—even the waves are flatter; central Florida, and you range from sugar cane fields and poverty to the cosmopolitan/Disney culture of Orlando and surrounding cities. And we can't forget the Keys, its two lane road cutting a swathe through the Gulf and Atlantic to Key West, home to Mallory Square's sunset festivities and the descendants of Hemmingway's six-toed cats.

Over the thirty plus years I've lived in Florida I've seen it move from a state reserved for the 'newly wed and nearly dead' to a growing culture of Cuban Americans, models and other trend setters, a younger population and more houses or condos cramming themselves into the rapidly diminishing lots of trees, fruit stands, and small family-run motels and businesses. In Southeast Florida, where I live, Spanish is heard far more often than English and larger businesses and banks require a certain number of staff to be bilingual. My hunch is that future Florida generations will grow up speaking both Spanish and English. My hunch also, somewhat tongue in cheek, is that Castro didn't need those long ago missiles to take over Florida. Cuba is already here, the very best of it hand in hand with the worst.

My poetry is a mixture of both inner and outer landscapes generated by the places I've lived and the people I've known in those places. Home has ranged from the South, Hawaii, the Mid-west, Manhattan, New England (Providence, RI and Boston, MA) and, of course, Florida. I've preferred to live by the sea (or on it, in the case of my six months on my 22 foot sailboat) and now, could never imagine living away from it. Each of those places has branded my heart in different ways and my poetry would be different had I not lived there.

Pris Campbell

Toast

Skin like burnt toast,
belly hanging over his embarrassed bikini,
the snowbird leers at the models
changing behind towels at South Beach.
He's as old as the Art Deco behind him
but his mind torques him back
to orange sherbet sunsets,
a pretty girl's hands tugging
his pants off in the beach sand,
the ocean's roar joining them
in oblivion.

His body was once shaped
taut like a sand sculpture
before the tide's gradual erosion,
carrying his manhood along with it.

The blare of cars trolling Collins Avenue
hides the thud of his heart when the model
eyes a dude on a skateboard, both still
unaware that the hands of father time
are sucking away their lives, just like his,
faster and faster.

Drifting

When the moon dozes, its
drift across South Florida
forgotten, he peeks
into my dream, worms
his way in. His presence
holds me hostage in REM,
eyelids fluttering.

Even the thunder from a storm
sweeping over from the Bahamas
fails to wake me.

He sweet-talks me, bids me
roll back the stone from
the tomb of old memories.
His breath becomes a song in
my ear, reminding me of what
used to be sweet and so
I open my arms, finally, to
say yes, to hold him, yes,
to bring it all back, but

he has already wandered away,
bored, to mess with some
other old lover's dream.

The Silence of Memory

Your car rumbles down the coast,
headlights searching the Daytona
skyline for your other life.

Memories erupt from a CD
and I appear, hand on your thigh.
A kiss, wet as the humid Florida air,
tickles one ear.

You brake, reach out to toss
aside my clothes, to fold
your body into mine, to draw
my breasts into your mouth until
you are filled with me, but

a pothole in the road startles.
The CD goes silent.
You rub your eyes to find
that only a strand of seaweed
marks my empty spot.

Feeding the Multitudes

Salvation Army full.
he drags a box into the park,
burrows beneath thick palms.
If the cops find him they'll
toss him out.

Other boxes breathe
in the darkness around him.

At least it's warm here in Florida.
Not like trying to survive
by lying on vents or navigating
the tunnels his year in Manhattan.

Dawn finally nudges.
His belly grumbles but
rain sprinkles make it unlikely
the commuters will be generous today.
He hikes to the ocean instead.

Barefoot in the surf, he pretends
he's Jesus, feeding the other homeless,
the discarded mentally ill, the displaced
Cubans, the disabled and elderly
with one tiny innocent fish.

Editor's Note: Mrs. Campbell was kind enough to offer a paragraph about each of her four featured poems. These well thought out offerings shed light on her creative process and most importantly: Why Florida speaks to her as an artist. I trust this will be an opportunity to articulate how environment can help shape us and help us to draw creative energy from our surroundings.

"Toast": In the eighties, my husband and I spent a weekend in an Art Deco hotel on Collins Avenue. Elderly locals played board games in the shade of awnings while models preened for the camera in bikinis and skate boarders whizzed by, along with hung-over revelers from a night in the many bars up and down the street. The contrast hits you in the face. The man in the poem grew from my imagination fueled by this scene.

"Drifting": Sometimes my ex visits my dreams. Our marriage ended in Florida, after our boat trip. Our relationship began going bad long before but the boat trip was one of the high points of my life. He had left a string of broken hearts before breaking mine. The trip made up for it all-- it was exhilarating.

"The Silence of Memory": How many of us have been involved with a man who was separated when we started seeing him only to see him return to his family, despite all of his initial intentions. I've been one of those women. I changed the name of the city for privacy, but I imagined him driving to his original home beside a tumultuous sea reflecting his churning emotions and mine.

"Feeding the Multitudes": The homeless increase in numbers in Florida when the weather changes up north. I'm basing this statement on my time working as a psychologist here and the influx of people with major mental illnesses into the treatment units seasonally. They live in the parks (if not caught), squat in empty buildings, set up boxes or makeshift tents in any remaining vacant lots with bushes. They stand on every major street corner with signs. I imagine one of them in this poem filled both with hope and delusion wandering to the ocean for sustenance, both for himself and the others.

COAST LINES:
FOCUS ON

HURRICANES

LeeAnn Kendall

My First Tropical Storm
by Beem Weeks

I'm a Michigander, born and raised. I'm used to cold winter months where the temperatures dip well below zero and the snow piles up by the foot. Summers in these northern climes can reach one-hundred degrees—though that's not often. The point is, I'm used to weather extremes. But nothing the Great Lakes state has to offer could prepare me for my Florida experience.

I re-located to Ft. Myers back in June of 1988. I'd needed a change of scenery, a new beginning, whatever you want to call it. A girl broke my heart—or I broke hers—and so the long trek from mid-Michigan to south Florida seemed the best remedy to soothe lost love. I had family there. My father, step-mother, and younger brother had made the move a year earlier. The journey made perfect sense to my 21-year-old mind.

Finding employment came easy. My father, having retired from General Motors, held a supervisor's position in a concrete pipe factory. Ft. Myers in the late 1980s was transitioning from cow town to booming metropolis. This expansion called for lots of concrete pipes for sewer systems and water drainage. I operated a forklift, taking pipes off the production line, loading them onto big rig trucks to be shipped to destinations all across south Florida.

The differences between Florida and Michigan are stark and immediate. Where Michigan is gray, cold and snowy at Christmas, Ft. Myers offered 75 degrees and sunshine. In Michigan, we'll see rain a few days each month. Grass and vegetation will often die and turn a brittle brown under the dry summer heat. But Ft. Myers sees rain pretty much every day—sometimes several times a day—which keeps the scenery green and fresh. There were even moments where the sun would be shining and the rain would be falling at the same time. We don't get that too often in Michigan.

Another thing we don't get in Michigan is the tropical storm. These massive storm systems are the precursor to hurricanes. In late 1988, I experienced my first—and only—tropical storm. Called Keith, this storm system dumped rain upon southwest Florida in amounts I'm sure Noah himself could certainly appreciate. Powerful winds whipped through the area, ripping roofs off many structures.

I remember working in the factory yard that day beneath a light but steady rain. Yellow rubber rain slicks covered me from head to toe—and still I found myself soaked to the bone. Late in the day the rain picked up strength, pelting me in the face, causing me to put on safety glasses to protect my eyes. I worked until ten o'clock that night, doing a job that normally had me clocking out around six o'clock. It would be past midnight by the time I arrived home.

All through the night the wind howled its threats against our house, promising to remove roof and siding with barely a thought. Rain spilled from thick, dark clouds that swirled across the sky like menacing gods. The power abandoned us sometime during the night, leaving us to candlelight and a battery-operated radio.

By first light the following morning the worst of the storm had passed. We were expected to report to work, just like any other day. Seems unless it's a full-fledged hurricane, it doesn't count for much with the boss man. But our entire neighborhood was under water. In our backyard, we had a boat canal. Across the street flowed the Caloosahatchee River. These two entities rose together, flooding the area, leaving houses—ours included—stranded like dozens of islands. And still, we were ordered to work—though the boss man had given us a few hours to make the thirty minute drive.

We survived. We even made it into work just before noon. Nobody else at the plant lived on the river, so flooding didn't hinder their travels, which made me and my father the only ones who were late that morning.

I've since moved back to Michigan. I just missed those familiar sights and the people with whom I grew up. But I still have a head full of memories of the nearly two years I called Ft. Myers home. I intend to one day return to south Florida—if only for a visit—just to see the changes that twenty-five years can lay on a city and its sights. And every year, right during hurricane season, when the storms begin their march toward dry land, I break out my story of Keith and the night I survived my first—and only—tropical storm.

Hurricane
by Ann Browning Masters

Ululations
to the builders
of condos on dunes,
to sand barons
who swear
that the ocean
never raves
beyond high tide.
Yet here we are,
witnesses called
to drive wrong-way
on a banshee beach,
to flap like crazed
hurricane angels,
stung to life
by lasers of sand.

We knew how
a beach house
should be raggedy.
We knew how
to love the wild mother
from a *distance*,
with tins of food
and pots of water,
pilau and pound cake
cooked to keep us
when the power went.
And we knew
how to leave
in the last crack
of drivable wind.

Hurricane Winds
by Gigi Mischele Miller

A wet maple leaf clings tightly to my cheek
Hurricane winds whisper & sing a thousand messages
Sent to anyone who would listen
Though I cannot seem to understand
I am sure they have something important to say

Tree limbs crack and bend in submission
The rain, karate chops of ice crystals, slashes sharply at my face
Angry and fierce—punishing me for my sins
Thunder booms, declaring justice. Stops. And starts again.
A nest of baby squirrels fall at my feet, shaken, like little children afraid of the dark

One, scurries up my leg, over my face, and then up, up and away
Back to his mother, somewhere hiding in the branches
His nails have scratched my face, which stings and burns,
Warm blood with cold rain, mixes hard on my face
Lightning blazes across the sky—a flash—a strobe light dancing, flying sparks

I wonder if it might strike at the mighty oak
That stands like a guardian over me
I think I see several eyes glowing, looking at me
Across the way—spotted just for a second, in the flash of light
The sky freezes, and it is bright like day

Time pauses, and the moment imprints itself in my mind
To whom do the eyes belong?
Fear seizes me
I am not in control of my destiny tonight

Debris flings past, as if carried by ghosts
I remember yellow foam skirting across wet sands in winter
When it is deserted, cold, grey and beautiful
The winds are strong and try to rip me from my oak
I hug harder to become one with my tree, and I pray

In the next flash of lightning, the eyes are gone
I am left now, truly alone, with the oak,
And the howling Wind
And the black sky
And the pellets of angry rain,
And I cling, alone … in Hurricane Winds

Impressions of Arthur
by Tovah Janovsky

    In late June we learned Hurricane Arthur was moving its way up the Florida coast. Bored, with nothing to do, my husband and I ventured out on July 2nd to witness its effects, as it began breezing past Flagler County. My senses soon became bombarded with images causing my brain to churn out a bit of free verse poetry. I found an envelope in my tote and quickly began jotting down these "Impressions of Arthur".

Cruising southward in our car on A1A, I look out at the brewing tempest.

Atlantic waves tipped their caps of white at the sun

I squinted at the golden sheen on the waves before they crested and crashed.

The sirens of the deep sang loudly, churning the waters above.

A canopy of inky grey skies hovered over the angry waters.

A smattering of ocean bathers risk safety to romp in the briny froth maybe just so they could say they did.

A senior couple on a beachside bench looked out, marveling in silence.

Seaside sago palms waved to each other, and chatted "Here we go again".

Ghost-town like roads and parking spaces beckoned to the cars to come and fill them.

The lifeguard rested on her perch, a silent sentinel looking out at the growing fury.

Was she staring at it in fascination or wondering if her boyfriend is cheating on her?

The ghost crabs hunkered down in their sandy caves in case things got dicey.

Western blue skies and white clouds rendezvoused with eastern grey skies and clouds sharing a kiss over Flagler Beach.

Driving home the blue skies surrendered their place to those of charcoal grey.

Drizzle splattered our windshield and soon turned to rain announcing Arthur's arrival.

Pelicans gracefully drifted by, unruffled by Arthur's presence as seagulls screeched their welcomes.

LET ME TELL YOU
A STORY:

FLORIDA FICTION

Rebecca Rousseau

At The Palms
by Bud Smith

We came back from the beach, carrying the empty bottle of tequila, the unused sun tan lotion, the wet towels, the radio.

there was a wedding about to start on the outdoor patio of our hotel. the stairs to our room were blocked by a man in a dark suit and dark sunglasses.

he'd have moved, of course, but I didn't feel like asking, and he didn't offer.

that's how life works sometimes.

so, not thinking clearly, we stepped into the pool, instead. and swam. and swam. and swam.

and on the patio, people seated in white slat chairs at the wedding, waited, waited for the bride, waited for cake, waited for someone to kick us out of the pool, but no one did. they all watched us swim, though, as if we were the opening act.

the sun fell too. that was the other nice part.

two security guards stood on the lip of the pool, arms crossed, watching us swim.

"come in," i said, "water's perfect."

not even a smile.

candles flickered. palm trees swayed. a golden moon rose over the hotel.

that's when the Wagner began, a small girl with an orange cello. and the bride proceeded past the pool, to the waiting crowd. and a hush was spread across the peninsula.

my wife and I bobbed in the deep end. humming along.

then we noticed the groom, with his white lily pinned to his tan tuxedo. he looked bullet proof. and the bride made it all the way across the flickering patio, and the Wagner stopped.

the priest began to talk, as priests are known to do, but we could not hear the priest.

so we swam again. slow laps. slow doggie paddle.

it didn't take long. the ceremony ended. a big kiss.

we clapped too.

"sooner or later, the whole wedding will wind up in this pool," my wife said.

"they'd be crazy not to."

"they'll jump right in, in their suits and everything."

"and the bride in her gown."

"and the security guards'

"all of them."

"it'd be horrible luck not to do that."

"exactly."

the DJ put party music on. my wife and I started to dance in the pool. the air cooled off outside and the water felt warmer. and warmer and warmer. but no one came in the pool with us. imagine that.

we danced all night in the pool, the wedding happening on the patio. us in the water, never getting out. and then the wedding ending. and the music ending. and the moon passed the center of the horizon and going back down into the sea. and us still swimming and dancing and laughing.

me pissing, and her pissing, I'm sure.

happiest, of anyone in florida.

Savages
by David Dannov

I was substitute teaching one day at some middle school in L.A., and during lunch, after I ate, returning back to my classroom, I came across a book written for that age, a kind of history book for kids.

The book told of many battles in Florida before the American Revolution.

Although I didn't live in Florida, I thought it was a good book.

It was written simple with an easy flow, and it didn't skip gory details.

I kept shaking my head, scowling, huffing, and laughing at the absolute absurdity of how many lives were lost for the control of power, how the Spanish stole land from the Indians, how the French stole land from the Spanish, and how pathetic it all was most Americans didn't know the actual history of their country, let alone the history of their own state.

As kids, we Americans learned the basics in public school: The American Revolution, George Washington, Ben Franklin, Abraham Lincoln, The Declaration of Independence, all that apple pie, patriotic crap. But once we graduated high school, got married, jumped into careers, had children, we didn't investigate the matter further buckled down by the everyday struggles of survival.

Thinking of this, recently single and tired of the boredom and loneliness that comes with the bachelor lifestyle of being a struggling writer in your thirties, I immediately thought of taking a road trip through Florida with a small camera crew and confronting residents regarding all this.

Eager to give the whole idea a shot, after explaining my idea, I asked a few friends who owned a good camera and knew about microphones and film editing if they'd like to join me on a one week crusade through Florida.

I'd pay for all the hotel and gas expenses if they were willing to buy their own food.

They agreed to come along, laughing and smiling, finding the idea original and daring.

Putting it together, rounding up what we needed, a small outline of events, a map, film equipment, and other financial necessities, we were off the following week ready to film it all and expose the inadequacy of American, public education and the ignorance of everyday American citizens, particularly on the subject of state history.

My first stop was a *Star Bucks* in Orlando, Florida confronting an employee of a local coffee shop.

With a pimple on the edge of his nose, not knowing what to say to me after I'd asked him a few questions on the history of Florida, this twenty-something employee blushed as he mentioned a rather boring detail about alligators.

Trying not to laugh, I asked him if he knew anything about the Indian tribes that once thrived in Florida before it was so-called civilized, tribes like the Apalachee, Ais, Caloosahatchee, Calusa, Jaega, Mayaimi, Tequesta, Tocobaga . . .?

He was silent, and then laughed, not able to comment, particularly after I'd told him the word *Tampa* meant *sticks of fire*, which came from the language of the Calusa tribe, referring to lightning continually plaguing the skies. He just nodded and kept clearing his throat, even after I told him the Indians in the Tampa area were warriors, that they fought bravely, not giving into Catholicism, and that the Spanish were unable to conquer them for two hundred some odd years after the Spaniards first arrival.

"Would you like a Mocha or what?" he finally asked me with angry eyes—sweat beginning to form on his forehead.

I didn't answer him. Instead I told him about Pánfilo de Narváezs' expedition. "Did you know," I began to ask him, holding the microphone to my mouth standing behind the coffee counter facing the guy with a smirk, "this Spanish explorer had sailed Florida's west coast in 1528?"

He huffed with a grin.

"Did you know Pánfilo was commissioned by the Spanish King, Emperor Carlos the Fifth to colonize the entire Gulf Coast?"

"Listen, man," he replied, frustration turning his face into a red, blushing mug. "I need to get back to work here. I've got things to do."

I glanced around the empty coffee shop.

Not a single customer.

Smirking, I said, "Okay, just one last thing."

He stood there, and shook his head with a sigh. "What?" he finally asked me.

My two camera crewman standing behind me getting it all on film chuckled lightly.

"Imagine yourself on this boat with Pánfilo, imagine what you would've seen, what the uncivilized coast of Florida might've looked like with all its wild, uncut vegetation."

"Why would I do that?" he replied as if I'd asked him to examine his asshole. Seeing me smile at him, he finally walked away and began mopping the floor behind the front desk counter.

It was time for our next destination.

About an hour and a half later, we ended up in a grocery store in Tampa Bay.

With the microphone ready, and the camera crew set, I randomly chose a customer near the front entrance of the store, having talked to the manager on duty, and getting his okay.

I wanted the manager to feel cozy in the illusion of being in control.

The customer's name was Aunt Emily, as she'd told me, and she was shopping for a new kind of hair spray she heard about from her friend Betsy.

I told her what I was doing there, and eventually mentioned the explorer Pánfilo again, and asked Emily if she knew this Spanish explorer held an Indian man hostage, and kidnapped him from his native shore eventually taking him aboard his ship.

She laughed, and embarrassingly tapped my chest with a smile. "No, of course not. I don't even know who you're talking about." She smiled with a slight blush.

"Okay," I chuckled. I told her who he was.

"Ucita?" she sarcastically asked. "That's the Indian's name?"

"Yeah. He was a native leader in a tribe that lived in this part of the coast."

"Oh, how interesting," she said, glancing around nervously. She wanted to get going. She had to get that hairspray.

"Before you go," I said to her, "I thought I'd mention one more thing."

She nodded and squinted. "Okay, uhhhh, what's that?"

"Well, poor Ucita wasn't treated so good on the ship. He was tortured, in fact, and Panfilo ordered his men to cut off his nose to find out where any hidden gold from his tribe was buried?"

The woman stood there as if she'd just shat her panties.

"Yep," I smiled, "This was the kind of guy he was, the father of Florida."

Aunt Emily's face took on a smiling grimace. "I have to go," she said, quickly walking off.

I stood there with a look of dumbfounded amusement.

106

A minute later, walking out of the store—my camera crew following and filming—I ran into Isabella who worked as a waitress in Fort Lauderdale visiting a pregnant friend down the street.

Her friend, she told me, had two children at the age of seventeen.

Introducing myself, and telling her my film idea, I asked her if she knew who Pánfilo was, if she knew about the various disasters befalling his expedition.

What do you know, she hadn't heard of him. Nor did she know his crew, consisting of 300 men, was reduced to four men from native attacks and disease.

"Wait a minute," she finally smiled at me. "I actually recognize that name. Is he that guy who met Colonel Sanders and came up with his costume?"

I stood there, stumped with a look of laughing shock. I waited for her to tell me she was joking.

But it never came.

"No," I finally said like a game show host speaking to one of the dumbest guests he'd ever had on his show. "He was an explorer who discovered the Gulf Coast."

"Oh," she smiled, chewing her gum.

I smiled trying to enjoy myself, relieved I was getting all this on film. "Actually, Pánfilo, trying to reach Mexico, eventually drowned when a storm capsized his boat?"

Isabella glanced around nervously, and said, "Okay, well, good luck with your film. Got a barbeque to get to. Sodas, chips, hot dogs, lots of things to buy." She walked toward the entrance of the store.

About ten minutes later I saw a man stepping out the grocery store wearing a suit. I stepped forward and introduced myself.

After hearing me explain my film project, he introduced himself to me.

He was the CEO of the Florida Gaming Corporation.

"No kidding," I said. "Okay, then you might just know who Álvar Núñez Cabeza de Vaca was."

He laughed. "Sorry about that," he smiled. "No, not exactly."

I told him Álvar Núñez was one of the four crewmen who'd survived Pánfilo's boating tragedy—Pánfilo being the Spanish explorer discovering the Gulf Coast.

"Okay," he grinned, nodding, embarrassed yet trying to understand.

After asking him what he liked to do in his spare time, finding out he was quite a gambler, playing the slots in one of the many casinos in Florida, trying not to bore the guy, I finally told him Cabeza eventually trudged between Florida and Mexico for nine years, and that he finally returned to Spain publishing his observations.

"My secretary might know some of this stuff," he said to me. "She loves history."

"Oh, great," I said, "Yeah, maybe she knows what the guy looked like."

"Maybe," he said, eventually giving me her cell phone number and telling me she'd appreciate the film idea.

An hour later, I was sitting on a bench in some local park, as my little crew of friends filmed me on the phone with the CEO's secretary.

"No," the secretary said—her voice routed directly into the camera recorded on tape. "I don't know who he is. But I do know those old, Spanish explorers had long beards."

"Okay," I laughed, coughing. Not wanting her to think I was making fun of her, I quickly said, "So did Cabeza, well, maybe not a huge beard. But I've seen an illustration of him. He seemed to have these kind and intense, almost tragic-filled eyes."

"Oh, how interesting."

"Yeah," I said, trying to be as genuine as possible even though I knew the woman didn't know a thing about the guy, "and he wore a circular hat with a jacket donning silver buttons and blousy shoulders."

She laughed. "That sounds like an explorer all right."

The conversation didn't go beyond the surface of clothing.

To save film, I cut the interview short.

A day later, ready to eat some food with my film crew, ending up in a drive-thru at some fast food place in West Palm Beach, I stuck out my head from the driver's window, told the employee who I was, what I was doing, and who Cabeza was in general.

One guy in the back seat had his camera facing the employee while I held the microphone to his mouth.

"Okay," he said, wearing a hat in the shape of a burrito, "So why are you telling me this?"

I smirked. "Well, I was just wondering if you could take yourself away from this job for a moment, take yourself back to Florida before fast food and gas stations, and imagine yourself with Cabeza on his journey."

The employee had a strange, hypnotic look in his eyes.

"Can you picture dragon-like crocodiles and abnormally large insects resembling goblins from the underworld?"

He stood there in a stupor. Then he walked away, as a manager appeared at the window. "Sir, this really isn't the time for this kind of thing."

"You're right," I said to the manager with a grin. "But since there aren't any cars behind me, and the place seems pretty empty right now." I could see the empty dining room through the drive-through window. "Let me ask one last question."

"Okay," he quickly smiled, amused by the camera facing him from the back seat window.

"Do you think the governor of Florida has any clue as to what kind of flora grew along the Florida coast before the Twentieth Century wrecking-balled its way in?"

He just stared at me with blank eyes. Then he asked, "What's 'flora' mean?"

I grinned, and shook my head. "Yeah, okay, sorry, it is vegetation."

He just stared at me again.

I grinned. "Do you think he'd know what kind of tribes Cabeza encountered during his personal explorations, tribes like the Karankawas, Atakapans, Caddoes, Jumanos, Mariames, Coahuiltecans, and the Zunis?"

He didn't comment. He just walked away, as his employee returned with our bags of food.

I paid the man, grabbed the bags, placed them on my buddy's lap in the passenger seat, placed the microphone atop some wrapped, warm food in an open fast food bag, grabbed the steering wheel, and took off—my camera crew laughing their asses off.

A few nights later, in a biker bar called Bubb's Fin and Feather, I ended up talking with a man wearing a white T-shirt having Jerry Garcia's smiling face on it.

He was donning a moustache and goatee with a skull and rose tattoo on his right arm. Hearing my film idea, and knowing the owner of the bar personally, he agreed to be filmed, and eventually met me in the patio section of the bar for a few questions. He was the first one in an interview who actually knew who Cabeza was.

I was ready to ask him a few questions when his girlfriend showed up.

She was smokin'-hot with tight jeans and perky breasts under a tight, pink T-shirt that read, "Blow Me, Jerk." Determined to get into the shot, she convinced her boyfriend to step aside and have me ask her the questions instead of him.

Why not, I figured.

After her boyfriend explained what I'd been talking to him about, who Cabeza was, all that, and even though it was obvious she wouldn't know the answer to the question I was about to ask, I asked her if she knew Cabeza had had sex with a native girl in his travels, and that he eventually had children with her.

She laughed, and said, "no, of course not." She chewed her bubble gum, and took a drag off her cigarette. Smirking, she finally said, "It doesn't surprise me though. Walking through the malls in this state you'll see all kinds of sexy ladies with dark skin and green, Spanish eyes." She laughed, and said, "Brook Hogan has green eyes. Just look at her."

"Who's that?" I asked her with a curious grin.

"Hulk Hogan's daughter."

"Oh, okay." I smirked, remembering the bulky, blond WWF wrestler from when I was a boy. "Does she have dark skin?"

She didn't respond, assuming I should know the answer.

"Well," I smiled, "do you think she knows who her great, great grandparents were?"

"I would hope so. Maybe they were Spanish. But I know Florida is filled with Italian descent as well."

She was pretty smart.

I was pleasantly surprised. "Okay, let's talk about something different, something relating to Florida's history."

"Okay," she smiled. "Go ahead."

"Hernando de Soto's invasion of Florida in 1539. Do you know anything about it?"

She laughed. "Uhhhh, what?"

I laughed too.

Her boyfriend huffed. Then he put his arm around his girl, and whispered something in her ear. He smirked, and said, "c'mon, Tracy."

I smiled. "Hey, she's actually not doing half bad. You should hear some of the answers people have been giving me so far."

They laughed, and drank their beers.

Eventually the boyfriend said with a grin, "Hey, I've got something for you."

I smiled. "Oh yeah? What's that?"

"This guy Hernando De Soto, the explorer dude you mentioned."

"Yeah," I smiled; amused he had something to say about him.

"I know about him because his description of the Indians was pretty racy. He called them, 'pagan devils incapable of ownership.' I always got a kick out of that."

His girlfriend laughed, as he proudly smiled, and said to her, "No shit, Tits."

He faced me with smiling wisdom, and added, "That's probably what led to the black-eyed, red-skinned, horned head, spear-carrying devil image we've all seen before."

I smiled and nodded. "You're right on target, I'd say." I switched the microphone from my mouth to his, waiting for his response.

He didn't volunteer anything.

So I added, "Those illustrated devils you're talking about began to appear in newspaper cartoons leading to European settlers coming up with the slanderous name, *Red Devils*, which eventually leaked into future, American baseball team names."

He laughed. "How 'bout that. My nephew's Little League team is named the Red Devils."

The next morning I talked to a gas station attendant somewhere in Orlando.

He was taking a break, drinking a cup of coffee near a rusty garbage can. It was 11:30.

The gas station attendant seemed annoyed a camera was facing him as I told him about Hernando de Soto and his invasion of the Florida coast.

Then I asked him about Lucille Ball, whether the famous actresses' grandchildren would have any idea who Tristán de Luna y Arellano might actually be.

He laughed and spit on the ground. With a smug smile, he asked me, "Who the fuck is Lucille Ball?"

I grinned. "'I love Lucy', ever heard of it?"

"No," he said with a furrowed brow, throwing his empty coffee cup in the trash next to him.

I smirked, and said, "Tristan was one of the Spanish explorers that helped discover the state of Florida. Forget about Lucy Ricardo."

"What in the hell are you talkin' about, man?"

"You know what, never mind. Sorry, this was a mistake." I motioned the film crew to head out.

He smiled, embarrassed, not sure what to say. "No, man. I gotcha'." He laughed. "You're just doin' your film thing."

The crew kept filming.

I nodded with a smile doing everything I could not to let this dickhead know I thought he was a complete idiot with major anger issues.

He stared at me, and nodded, motioning for me to continue with my questioning.

"Go ahead, man. It's cool."

I stared at him for a moment, trying to decide whether I should leave or actually waste my time standing there continuing to interview this prick. "All right, well, uhhhh, this guy Tristan established a settlement in Pensacola. But it was abandoned in 1561."

"Another history lesson. Damn, Dude. I feel like I'm in grade school."

I didn't know what to say.

"I didn't care about history when I was a kid, and I don't care now. Why would you think I give a shit about your lame-ass film project?" He faced the camera with a seething grin.

"Well," I smiled, switching the microphone to my mouth, "Like I told you before, I'm here to find out how educated the locals are of their own state's history. You're making it pretty clear. Thanks for that."

"Oh," he said, stepping closer to me with tightened fists, "so you're tryin' to make me look like a dick is that it?"

"No," I said. "You're doin' a great job of that yourself." I hesitated. I wasn't sure what to say next without this guy possibly getting violent. "Look," I finally continued, "I'm just makin' a film. That's all. Instead of getting all pissed off about it why not try and put yourself in those Spanish explorers' shoes. They certainly went through some heavy shit." I huffed, and shook my head, "I mean, c'mon, man, you're standing here in your gas station attendant uniform acting all bent out of shape and those explorer guys had to tough out Indian attacks, crocodiles, no air conditioning, often times foraging and hunting their own food. So instead of playing tough, why not open your mind a little and imagine yourself on one of those early, seventeenth-century ships having to eat raw meat with maggots on a creaking ship weeks before it arrived here in Pensa Cola. Who knows, you might like yourself for it."

He stood there and stared at me as if asked him to pick up the dead body of an alien. Knowing he had nothing to offer, he finally resorted to insults, "Get a life, man. You're dumbass, film project sucks all the balls of all those explorers you keep talking about. So why don't you take that microphone and shove it up your ass before I do it myself?"

I smiled shaking my head, not wanting to fight. Sighing, I walked to the rented car in the parking lot with my small camera crew, and immediately took off. Driving, imagining that asshole as one of the crewman of Tristan's ship, I laughed, picturing him shitting his pants in a shadowy, ship corner adding to his smell of body odor and piss from months being at sea. Then I thought about another explorer who'd helped discover Florida.

He was some French guy who went by the name René Goulaine de Laudonnière. I knew this from reading about him this very morning before leaving the hotel. I learned he founded Fort Caroline in 1564. In mid-thought, I winced seeing one of the film crewmen from the back seat surprise me with a camera in my face. I laughed and huffed. "What are you guys doin'?"

Holding the microphone to my mouth, pretending to be me, he asked me, "Did you know Rene wrote a book about his experiences?"

"Yes," I smiled into the camera, "I did, Jerry." I cringed, knowing he was trying to give me a dose of my own medicine, perhaps empathizing with some of the people I interviewed. Perhaps he felt I was expecting too much of them.

Continuing my answer, I said. "As a matter of fact, Jerry, I know he called his book, *His Histoire notable de la Floride.*"

Just out of college, working as a waiter, Jerry didn't say anything for a moment. Then he said, "You only know that because you've been studying up on the state."

"Okay," I said. "You got me. I'm a recent student of Florida's history. At least I'm studying up on it though. What's wrong with that?"

"You wouldn't even know any of the answers to your own questions if you didn't look it up before asking them?"

I smiled, looked down, shook my head in defeat, and sighed. "Maybe you're right. Maybe I'm just as clueless as some of these people I'm interviewing. It's just dates and names of ghosts no longer remembered. Who cares, I guess."

He didn't say anything.

The other cameraman, George, a chubby and bright journalism major intervened, and said, "Wait a minute. I think you're onto something here with this project. You're just trying to make a point."

I asked him with a hopeful grin, "What point am I making, George?" I modestly shrugged my shoulders. "That we're all idiots?"

They both laughed.

"No," he finally smiled from the back seat, sitting next to Jerry. "that we should know the history of our country, let alone the history of own state? You're not from Florida, and neither are we? Maybe we should know more about it, but these people from Florida should know at least a little of their own state history. I mean, I know California's history pretty good."

I didn't say anything. I couldn't help but smile. I felt better thanks to George. Then I asked the two of them, "Oh, hey, by the way, did you guys know the colonists in this Florida region we're driving through at this very moment were antagonized by local natives?"

"Oh no," Jerry said. "Now he's doing it to US?"

I laughed. "No, I'm just asking. From what I understand, many of these guys on the ship eventually refused to work, while others took to piracy, even mutinying in the end."

They didn't say anything.

"Is that what's going on here, Jerry?" I asked him this with a grin, "A mutiny?"

He didn't comment.

"No, sorry," Jerry finally said, taking the microphone away from my face. "I'm just playin' around, man."

"Okay, then, what do you say we save tape for the last few interviews."

George turned off the camera and nodded his head with an embarrassed huff.

The following day, after making a few phone calls, we ended up driving to an elementary school in Jacksonville.

I was allowed to interview a secretary at the front desk, especially it being so early in the morning before students and most teachers arrived.

Her name was Miss Loggens, a black woman at least a hundred pounds overweight.

"So," I said, holding the microphone and standing on the other side of that front desk counter, my film crew recording behind me, "Have you heard of Pirate Hawkins."

"Yes," she laughed. "He was that pirate that stole all that gold wasn't he?"

"Uhhh," I smiled, trying not to laugh. "Yeah, kind of. He also captured slaves off the West African coast even though Spanish prohibition was in full force. He eventually met up with a Spanish explorer named René."

This was the same René I'd been talking about for days so I felt it was relevant.

"Pirate Hawkins sold René a boat," I rambled on, "so he could sail back to France apparently."

"Oh," Miss Loggins smiled, "Like I told you on the phone, you need to talk to Mr. Hoover. He's the History Teacher here. He loves this stuff."

"Great," I smiled. "Is he in yet?"

"Yes, he arrived an hour ago. He always comes in early. You can go visit him if you like. He called me earlier and told me to tell you can go to his room anytime."

Getting an okay to film on campus by the Principal of the school, I immediate went to Mr. Hoover's classroom.

"Hello," he smiled, as he opened his classroom door. He was a heavyset man with a stoic jaw and piercing eyes. Wearing a yellow polo shirt and jeans, he said to me, "They phoned me a few minutes ago and told me you'd be here."

"Is it okay we talk for a half hour or so?" I asked him.

My camera guys were holding their equipment behind me, already filming.

"Sure," he smiled, "I've got a Conference this period so it worked out perfect."

"Oh, great," I said, knowing a Conference period meant a free period, as I'd substitute taught in L.A. Unified for years. I waved to the boys to follow me into the classroom, as I walked in and glanced around the room.

The classroom had all kind of cool posters of American events on the walls—The America Revolution, The Civil War, The Great Depression, the Industrial Revolutions.

I already liked this guy.

Eventually setting up the camera equipment near Mr. Hoover's desk, sitting in front of him, I told him all about my film project, why I was doing it and my experience so far—the film crew in the background recording it on tape.

He laughed, and said, "Oh, man, yeah, that's gonna' be tough trying to get people you don't even know to participate, especially about history. For the most part, people don't want to know history because history requires you to memorize. And to memorize takes effort."

"Okay," I smiled. "I can see that. But still, even if you don't know dates, which isn't my expertise either, you could at least know some basic things that went down in your own state?"

He laughed, especially because I'd already shown him some film footage of some various interviews.

He'd thought the project was hilarious.

"You know," he went on after I got back to filming him, "this guy Rene you're talking about in the film, he had to answer to charges of sedition in France, or should I say, 'anarchistic thought,' and his departure to France was delayed by the appearance of the Spanish."

"Finally," I smiled, "someone who knows more about this stuff than me." I glanced at the camera crew, and said, "And I only know about it because I'm reading about it as I go along."

He smiled and laughed. "I gotcha'. Okay, let's see if I can give you something you can use."

"Actually," I politely interrupted, "I have a question to ask you first if you don't mind?"

"Oh, okay, yeah, sure, go ahead, shoot."

I grinned and nodded. "When did the French get involved since Florida was primarily a Spanish discovery?"

He smiled and nodded. "Great question," He cleared his throat. "Are you aware of the French King, Charles the Ninth?"

"Never heard of him."

He laughed. "Okay, he was a sickly King. He suffered from a blood disease in his early twenties."

I smiled. "Sounds like most European Kings to me, eating gold and swallowing land thinking it was a good diet."

Mr. Hoover laughed. "I like your sense of humor, Marcus." He nodded and coughed. "In a way you're right. He was competing with the Spanish for territory in Florida already inhabited by the Indians."

I huffed and shook my head. Then I said with a cocky smile, "Two hyenas trying to steal a bear's meal from his own cave."

He laughed again and nodded. "Except they really believed they had the right to take the land under the Indian's feet." He said this with a grin.

I squinted and smirked. "Well, it WAS Manifest Destiny after all. God's given right to take whatever they wanted, right?"

He laughed, knowing these wealthy, elite, dickheads from our American past used Manifest Destiny as some kind of twisted justification for stealing land from the Indians so the masses wouldn't get upset enough for rebellion. "It sure was." He was quiet for a moment. Then he said, "you know, my grandfather's house was built near the same land where Pedro Menéndez de Avilés, the Spanish explorer I was talking about, attacked Fort Caroline and massacred most of those left by the French."

"No kidding."

Mr. Hoover nodded, excited to be telling this to someone actually listening.

"Pedro took over San Augustín, which is really Saint Augustine now, one of the oldest, inhabited, European settlements in any U.S. state."

"How 'bout that, a person who knows Florida history. It took a history teacher, I guess."

"It's my job. I better know some things."

I laughed. "Thank God we ran into you, Mr. Hoover. I was beginning to lose hope in America."

He laughed. Then he started talking about the Spanish culture, what the Spanish explorers wore, and what they looked like.

I grinned, and said, "What's crazy to me is the fufu outfits these explorers often wore, like those frilly, white collar things you'd picture a dog in a circus wearing, and those shirts that looked like blouses—wigs and all." I laughed. "They almost dressed like clowns."

"Yes," he agreed, smiling, "and combine all that with their rugged skin and facial hair, and I'd say they were a paradox to see, especially to the Indians."

I laughed, and said with a grin, "Let me you ask you something, Mr. Hoover." I coughed, and cleared my throat, unable to stop grinning. "If I went to Disney World right now and then

117

talked to some employee working one of the rides asking him if he knew anything about the Spanish Empire building Catholic missions in Florida do you think he'd have any idea what I was talking about?"

He huffed and smiled.

I grinned, and asked him, "Or maybe if I was more specific, and mentioned how, in 1565, Menéndez de Avilés attacked Fort Caroline killing almost all the French soldiers defending it, renaming the fort San Mateo, do you think he'd be able to contribute anything to the conversation?"

Mr. Hoover smiled.

I smiled back. "Okay, I'll take that as a no."

He just kept smiling. Then he said, "Hell no. They wouldn't know diddly. They wouldn't know any of this stuff you're talking about. Nor would they know anything about Dominique de Gourgues, a French soldier who tried to land on this very shore of Florida thronged with war-like Indians. They'd have no idea those Indians were at war with the Spaniards at Saint Augustine."

I nodded, a bit taken back, as I wasn't aware of what he was talking about.

"What about Miami call girls," he went on in the same way I'd been speaking in the video, mimicking my style, "I mean, they wouldn't ever, in their entire adult lives, consider what it was like to be on one of those early, Spanish ships, or to be on the very ship as Dominique de Gourgues witnessing all the violent movements of natives warning them not to land." He laughed again, and said, "You know, there's this story I love to tell my students every year having to do with the crew of de Gourges."

I smiled. "What's that?"

"It's about this Frenchmen who rowed a small boat from de Gourges' ship to the shore of this coast. He was heading toward that throng of angry Indians I mentioned, even with all that danger around him, even with all that jumping up and down with spears, feathers, and war paint."

I smiled and nodded.

In a burst of excitement, he kept his story going by saying, "One of the Indians in all that maddening frenzy shouted to the boat approaching them. He shouted this Frenchman's name, in fact, remembering him from years past, remembering him being a trumpeter from the French army. And good thing he did because his life was spared when he made it to shore because of it."

"Nice," I grinned, nodding. "That is a good story."

He nodded, smiling back. "The native Indian who greeted this French trumpeter spoke French from the many years the French had been there before, asking him why he'd left them, why he hadn't come back sooner. Then he mentioned there hadn't been a happy day since the French left them." He nodded and smiled. "And you know what? I happen to believe him."

"Impressive," I said, nodding like an auto shop student learning how to put together the detailed wiring of an engine, "that's pretty cool history, Mr. Hoover."

"Yeah," he agreed. "Imagine De Gourgue's relief once he knew his men could arrive on the shore in peace. It must've been something to see for sure."

I nodded with a smile, enjoying how this man had so easily taken over my role in the film and reversed it on me.

It was classic.

I eventually wound up the interview.

"Listen," Mr. Hoover said to me, "all in all, people don't have a clue when it comes to history. It's a sad thing. But it's the truth." He took a deep breath as if he was about to address an audience, and said, "let me put it this way. In the same vain as YOUR approach, Marcus ..."

He smiled, and said, "I doubt Triss, a teenage dog walker strolling down a St. Petersburg sidewalk would have any idea how Florida got its name."

I smiled, enjoying the guy's humor. Then I said with an embarrassed grin and a slight shrug, "Wait, I don't want to sound like Triss here, Mr. Hoover, but how *did* it get its name?"

He smiled and huffed. "From the Spanish term 'Pascua' which means 'flowery Easter' coined by Juan Ponce de Leon."

"There ya' go. Now that's something I should know given all the research I've done."

"Hey, that's okay. I don't know nearly as much about California than I do Florida." He coughed again. "I do know, however, De Gourgues talked to the powerful chief Satouriona, and that he became friends with the guy." He huffed with a smile, staring at the classroom rug. "You know, thanks to De Gourgue's fast talking, all of those Frenchmen greeting his warriors were most likely spared. But," he continued, "it would take an extraordinary person to even understand what an incredible moment that was. Most people need to see it in film to even visualize something as powerful as this. They need to see a scene of it in detail with costumes and actors in a movie, to actually see Satouriona sending word to all neighboring chiefs to meet the French, and to see, by the next morning, how a great council was held where all arms were laid aside."

"Yeah," I grinned, "films are good teachers. Unfortunately, I don't make movies."

He nodded. "That's not what you do. You're doing something different. You're proving a point. You're proving how a three hundred pound mother watching television in her Florida home would have a difficult time picturing Satouriona and De Gourgues sitting side by side on a seat decorated with gray moss while Indians and French warriors gathered around each other in a circle."

I laughed. "Good point. You should write a book about this guy Satour ..." I hesitated, having difficulty pronouncing his name.

"Satouriona."

"Yeah," I smiled, "that guy."

Mr. Hoover laughed, knowing I was giving him the floor. Then he sighed with a smile as if he'd been waiting for someone like me to give him a stage to vent, eventually talking about the Spanish robbing the Indians of food, driving them from their homes, and killing their children, all because they loved the French.

I kept nodding.

"There really is a movie to be made here," I finally said. "Maybe you should write the script."

He nodded with a grin. "I might just do that."

"Keep going, Mr. Hoover. Any final thoughts for the ending of my little documentary?"

He laughed. "Look, Marcus, I think you'd have to agree with me. Even though there are educated people in Florida and even across the States, on the whole, on a day to day basis, most Americans don't think beyond what freeways to take or what to have for dinner, not taking into account how the world they live in was ever forged."

I asked the boys to cut the tape at that moment, feeling it was an excellent way to end the film.

After thanking Mr. Hoover, telling him I'd send him a copy of the documentary when it was edited and ready to distribute, on the drive home, sitting in the driver's seat in silence listening to the hum of tires, I realized I needed one final clip to summarize it all into a proper ending.

It was at that moment when I imagined myself saying into the camera, "Of course, there's so much more that occurred in this state, no doubt more murder, violence, and suffering, horrible stories of torture and human tragedy. And what boggles the mind is that Florida is just one of the states out of fifty in this warring country. And they all have pasts filled with remarkable tales, despicaple battles, and loss of life. Mississippi, Colorado, Pennsylvania, North Carolina, Ohio, Texas, New Mexico. Alaska … it goes on and on, the blood from the creation of one single state.

Combine the states together and there'd be enough blood to fill the Great Lakes and possibly the Arctic Ocean. They don't mention *that* in the Star Spangled Banner now do they?

I imagined the documentary cutting out, as credits rolled with a last shot of me and the boys driving down the freeway at sunset listening to Muddy Waters sing, Deep Down in Florida as the colonial reddish-orange sun bled on the twilight, modern-grid, Florida horizon.

Ginna Wilkerson

100 THOUSAND POETS
FOR CHANGE
SEPTEMBER 27, 2014:

LOCAL OBSERVATIONS

Jeremy Jusay

100 Thousand Poets for Change – Saint Augustine
by Chris Bodor

Authors and poets, by design, are forced to spend many hours by themselves, in isolation engaged in the act of banging on their keyboard and crumbling paper. Once in a while we come out of our writing cubicles to observe, socialize and participate in life. During these hours in our creative writing cocoons, powerful words are often composed. Musicians like Bob Geldolf (founder of the Live Aid movement) and poet Bob Dylan are but a handful of the few humanitarians who have been able to write words that ignite change with those words alone. Can you imagine what would happen if all the poets of the world came out of their self-imposed isolation, for one day, under the umbrella of change?

The idea of solitary writers uniting on one day was the motivation for Michael Rothenberg to create a Facebook event invite a few years ago called 100 Thousand Poets for Change. He invited everyone he knew and encouraged them to invite everyone they knew. According to the movement's office web site, www.100tpc.org, more than 700 local observations were announced and archived in 2014. Twenty of them happened in Florida: Delray Beach, Ft. Lauderdale, Hogtown, Hollywood, Key Largo, Miami, Orlando, Palm Beach, Panama City Beach, Pensacola, Pompano Beach, Saint Augustine, Saint Petersburg, Tallahassee, Tarpon Springs, Titusville, West Palm Beach, Winter Haven and Winter Park

The 2015 global observation has been scheduled for Saturday September 26.

Everyone has a voice. Your thoughts are valid. Thank you to everyone who celebrated here in Saint Augustine with our four local 2014 events. The Ancient City Poets got on the bill at the Florida Heritage Book Festival with a panel discussion on change in downtown Saint Augustine at Flagler College. It was an ideal high-profile opportunity to kick-off a weekend of change. The spirit flowed to the Downtown Bazaar where the poets where given three ten minute slots on the main stage, in between each musical act. The next day featured a Poets for Change writing workshop led by Ann Kiyonaga-Razon and we wrapped up the weekend with a standing room only Poetry Reading for Change.

It was an amazing opportunity to come together to create, perform, educate and decide our own specific area of focus for change within the overall framework of peace and sustainability, which co-founder Michael Rothenberg stated, "…is a major concern worldwide and the guiding principle for this global event."

Change
by Michael Henry Lee

Originally the following senryu poem (a first cousin of haiku) was written in response to a news article on "climate change", also known as "global warming". It was first published in the January 2013 issue of Haiku News.

climate change
another sweater goes
to Goodwill

On a conscious level, a description of climate change was the initial objective. In Japanese poetry, brevity and open-endedness are of essential importance. I was looking for an element of this "global warming" phenomena that fit both the Japanese sensibility of brevity, and above all allowed the reader an open-endedness to draw their own conclusions and feel their own feelings.

Much to my delight somewhere between the conscious and subconscious writing process a poem was birthed that not only wound up being open-ended for the reader but the writer as well. Climate change, action, inaction, charity, apathy, motivation, all up for interpretation; a stance, a stand, a change.

Change Two
by Gayl *Angela* Masson

Resounding, pounding, bleating
the planets pull apart
unchained
no barrier explained.
That critical path of change
we're tied, unified,
to this cosmic constant
yet blind to the path
deaf to that bleating
of our planet depleting.

Let's change.
Let's wake up.
Each single one
and get a grip
on what we've done.

What can I do?
Just on my own?
How can I change?
To save our home?

Let's define
the range of hope
so we're not
strangled by the rope
we've hung
ourselves
let's change.

Just Yesterday
by Bozena Helena Mazur-Nowak

just yesterday she stood at the window
and watched as the life passed by
wilting flowers left in the pots
she no longer squints her eyes at the sun

shutters are still wide open
yellow plaster crumbles from the wall
at the bus stop grim obituary
whispers silent prayer for her soul

yesterday she greeted with a smile
today she adorn memories with tears
she helped the homeless and the hungry
she shared slices of bread out of love

she shared the crumbs with pigeons
little sparrows, squirrels, and cats
who will care for the sad little flock
which misses her sky-blue eyes

yesterday she stood at the window

Change
by Beverly Kessler

The word "Change" is elusive
With only implications of the truth,
Yet, is often used instead
To attract our naive youth.

No explanations are expected,
No details to critique,
Just a catchy word to draw you in,
So you don't have to think.

"Change" can lose your money.
"Change" can lose your wife.
"Change" can lose your job.
"Change" can lose your life!

This word is overused
By politics, media and such,
To deliberately cover up the facts
We need to hear so much.

We must become aware
Of just how vague a word can be.
Not to mention the destructive facades
Such as: "Change," "Choice," and "Transparency."

How shallow have we grown,
Allowing our society to be squeezed
And robbed of precious freedoms
By political charlatans and thieves?

The media's driven by your response
For monetary gains,
Continually twisting and turning these words,
This politicizing must be refrained!

Our economic debt is ruining us;
In Benghazi, we left our Ambassador to burn
Will Obama Care be America's "Change"
For us never to return?

Hitler "Changed" Germany
The Ayatollah "Changed" Iran.
Obama's "Fundamental Change"
Could be America's last stand.

Wake up Americans!
Or our history will report
That we only survived 240 years—
Your patriotism is our last resort.

Healing
by Robert Waldner

Do not cry for what's been lost
Do not cower in fear for what is to come
Change cannot be born of irreverence
We are not too broken to heal
Change is more than minted metal
It is greater than any arsenal of firepower
Healing is present
In the artist
Who feeds the bellies and souls of his community
And imparted by the poet
Who draws crowds in the name of his passion.

Progress is alive
In the independent publisher
Who bestows upon the world
The words of those who inspire him
Change is born of inspiration
Healing is born of change.

We are not too broken
To heal.

Presto
by Kurt McGill

All over the world
strangers only talk
over the weather
the broke-dick weather.
It's the same, the same.
Interchangeable.
Clocks forward
or backward.
When was that?
Blood moon.
That moment.
Make it stand still.
You wanted to see.
They stack the rubble
and throw it into the sea.
I've forgotten about it.
Washed up on the shore.
Hit-and-run over the loner
on the psycho road to hobo
a wet plastic bag in his hand.
Float him out on the ebb tide.
Let it all devolve onto me.
But not right now.
I used to live here but
I can't recognize anything
I deserve a cigarette.
Stop.
It's forbidden to walk there.
Say something!
On the landmine.
Has that been taken care of?

Change
by Ann Kiyonaga-Razon

background remains the same
ground of being...

foreground appears to change

change can challenge

disruptions
altered plans
new culture
different language

something in us
accepts this challenge, though
rising up
opening mind and heart
to the new

like a bird adrift
on myriad patterns of wind

a leaf circling downward as autumn dictates
this letting go

we slide and glide with what is offered

welcoming
passing seasons
growing older
the fluidity of it all

for we are anchored in our ground of being
the changeless at the heart of all fluctuations

change reveals the changeless

it's greatest gift and grace

this gift and grace inherent
in our changing world...

Seasonal Awakening
by Rachel Layne

Change is strange and sometimes necessary
Autumn develops
A sweet sense of liquid motion
Casting spells of deep dreams in the sky.

Why do we change?
Why is it strange?

The beauty is among us
The first leaf falls and it has begun
Gleaming slowly, I can see the sun.

The ocean breeze
Becomes light and chilly,
Yet it's still alive.

Change is strange and sometimes necessary,
Grab the whiskey and eggnog
We will surely survive!

Halloween and pumpkin pie
Get the little ones
Dress up and play
Family time is on the way!

Change is strange and sometimes necessary,
But all the memories are here to stay!

FLORIDA WRITES:

BOOK REVIEWS

Alex Boardman

Eve's Garden
Glenda Bailey-Mershon
ISBN: 978-940189-04-8
408 pages

Review by: Leny Kaltennecker

Eve's Garden is Glenda Bailey-Mershon's first novel. She grew up in the Appalachian South in a family with diverse roots. She has taught woman's studies, anthropology, history writing and GED preparation. She named the Ancient City Poets poetry reading group and has edited or co-edited four volumes of Jane's Stories Anthologies by woman writers. Her publications include **Sa-co-ni-ge** and **Blue Smoke**: **Poems from the Southern Appalachians**.

Her first work of fiction is based on a childhood world of Romani and Scottish family background where small minded people are not used to anyone who appeared different. Her novel describes growing up and the slow acceptance of these differences between all people. The Romani background, mostly hidden, is revealed little by little to an inquisitive child. The time period is set in in the Nineties – an old fashioned time for those not yet affected by 1969 and the Summer of Love. The Seventies depicted in **Eve's Garden** was a time where sex is a forbidden subject and never talked about. The silence evolves into a tragedy involving Eve's grand-daughter's best friend. The book meanders back and forth between the Seventies and the early Twentieth Century when slowly the secrets are revealed.

Glenda Bailey-Mershon uses a poetically lush language and carries the readers along the old, sometimes tragic, road of a family history, from past to present. It is difficult to put this book down. May I suggest that you set aside a leisurely weekend to enjoy this wonderful story.

The Ocean Highway at Night
Tim Gilmore
ISBN: 978-1497321724
161 pages

Review by: Charlie Cawley

In an interview, the author Ian McEwan defines his reverence for life in terms of "The little spark we do have." This I understood as our all too brief time on this planet as a gift we are given to love, to feel, to see and to share with others those various aspects of being. Those of us who are fortunate manage to express this "reverence" as artists, choosing from an array of mediums I can only define as infinite.

A great proportion of my existence in this "little spark" has been spent practicing the art of photography. In this time I've realized that the underlying, driving force behind what I do, has to do with sharing with others the visual delights the world serves up to my particular vantage point. I often feel the images I make are implicitly posing the question "Does the world really look like this?" The term "visual delights" has, over the course of my work morphed into a sense of awe for the gift of the encounter with the appearances I get to record. There are those times when the shutter clicks and my soul screams out a fist-pumping "Yes!" There is no need for a glance at the image on the proof sheet or the digital sensor to know I have been given the appearance as a gift. There's no other word for my sense of these encounters than the word awe, and the opportunity to share it with others is the sweet luscious icing.

At the front of the book **Florida Speaks**, Editor Chris Bodor wrote "With poems, instead of cameras, poets take snapshots of life." Now it would be easy for a photographer such as myself to take offense at this, but what Chris is referring to is a process similar to what I do, but in a different artistic medium. Art is, in its most simplified essence, putting things together. As a photographer I put encountered appearances together in the camera frame to create an image. A writer puts words together on a page. A dancer combines body movements to express emotion on a stage. A painter assembles brush strokes and colors on a canvas. A musician creates song from notes, voice and differing instrument sounds.

So it is with Tim Gilmore's book **The Ocean Highway**, an assemblage of elegant prose and bits of poetry, occasional photographs, creating snapshots of times, loves, histories, and places centered geographically on highway A1A south from Matanzas Inlet in the area of a place known as Summer Haven, south to "Marineland Dolphin Adventure" and, Washington Oaks Park Beach.

Gilmore creates snapshots of time with his description late 19th century Summer Haven as "plots of sand and hardscrabble," or "an oasis in the desert beside the sea." Summer Haven's principal citizen is a recluse referred to as the "Mayor of Summer Haven", often hovering about in the stories under various guises like some contemporary photo-bomber. The existence of Summer Haven is of course dominated by the grace and the often vicissitudes of the sea. "You should worry if you buy a house on the coast." Gilmore writes "Here the sea supersedes history. As though we have always been here. Long before we were here." Gilmore's early written snapshots of Summer Haven create an idea of a beach community we might all wish we could have grown up in. "We walked in the past looking for a present moment that would remain such for us." and a snapshot of that first and eternal love is created, through reminiscences of times in Summer Haven.

And, oh what a magnificent depiction of human folly Gilmore creates with his collage of writings and photographs of "Marineland Dolphin Adventure!" (Google map name for it!) Jaques Cousteau has commented that expecting to learn about marine mammals while observing them in captivity is like thinking that an anthropologist might believe he can learn about humans, by studying those locked in prisons. The inanity of this belief is spelled out in a story about a captive shark that, by the second day of captivity had given birth to 5 pups, ate 2 of them and died. Another story recounts a dolphin calf eating so much eel grass planted in the tank he died of indigestion. Then there was the manta ray that died because he was force fed fish rather than the shrimp and smaller creatures that form the staples of the manta ray diet. You have to ask "Who do we think we are?" when you read these stories. But despair not—there is humor in the story about Butch the California sea lion's two escapes and escapades to Miami. But Butch was finally lured back by a captive female sea lion named Fanny, both of whom disappeared with no record of where they went.

I do think though that a special part of this book resides in Gilmore's stories about his time spent in the coquina formations on the coastal side of Washington Oaks State Park. I've had the opportunity to spend some time there, photographing the formations, tide pools, sea grasses, cairns and craters, carefully stepping, climbing and jumping through it all. I say carefully because when there, I must constantly observe one of Ted Orland's Photographic Truths: "Camera lenses are attracted to rocks!"

Reading Gilmore's accounts of this surreal seascape has, however, brought me to a revelation of sorts regarding the limitations of artistic mediums. With a camera I can show you the grandeur of places such as this, but I cannot tell you how it feels. We can look at a print of Ansel Adam's Yosemite Half Dome and marvel at the magnificence, but we don't have a clue about what he was feeling at the time, unless we have access to what he might have written in his daybook entry. Gilmore, camera-like, can describe what his vision records with the words "Rock so smooth it organizes itself in arcs and curves and concentric layers yet rough with pockmarks and scars and pits and grooves." But the crucial aspect of his experience of this place sings out in words like "Watching the tides, he feels as small as one drop of a crash, with the difference that he's conscious of his existence. So he resurrects his worth in infinite loneliness. Does declaring it save his soul? Or does he even need to be saved in the context of such wonder? He thinks he'll let wonder and beauty save him, save him even from the need to be saved." I love the times when I read a writer's words and think "How does he or she do that?" My camera sure can't do that. Such is the distinction of the varying forms of art.

Initially I started with an artist's appreciation of the existential gift of awe coming into our lives and influencing the direction and drive for the artist's oeuvre. I'm convinced that Gilmore gets this too, as the word "awe" occurs in this book. No giveaway here though. To find it, I suggest you read it – with care.

CONTRIBUTORS

Editor's Note: Biography information on the three featured haiku writers: Michael Henry Lee, Antoinette Libro and Paula Moore appears together with their work, in The Haiku Mind section.

Glenda Bailey-Mershon grew up in the Appalachian South in a family with diverse roots, and now lives in North Carolina and Florida. Her publications include **sa-co-ni-ge**: blue smoke: poems from the Southern Appalachians; **Bird Talk: Poems**; A History of the American Women's Movement: a Study Guide; and four volumes as editor of Jane's Stories' anthologies by women writers, including **Bridges and Borders** (2013). She has been a finalist in Our Stories fiction contest; featured author at the Illinois Book Fair; and a grant recipient from the Illinois and Florida Humanities Councils, as well as the Florida Division of Cultural Affairs. **Eve's Garden**, her first novel, was recently published and is reviewed in the inaugural issue of A.C. PAPA.

Larry Baker is the author of five novels, four of which are set in or around Saint Augustine. His first, **The Flamingo Rising**, was an LA Times "Top 100" books of the year selection in 1997, and it was adapted by Hallmark for a television movie in 2001. His novel **A Good Man** was nominated for the Southeastern Independent Booksellers Association "Book of the Year" in 2010. His new novel, **The Education of Nancy Adams**, is set in the fictional north Florida town of Fort Jackson.

Carolee Ackerson Bertisch is the former Writing Coordinator of a New York School District, Poetry Chair of the Florida Heritage Book Festival, leader of two lively book discussion groups and was honored with the ROWITA Award for Women in the Arts by the St. Johns County Cultural Council in 2014. She is the author of two books of poetry and prose, **Who Waves the Baton? Musings about Nature, Life and Mountain Ranges**, and **Walking to the Beat, Life: Mystery, Melody and Motion**.

Nancy Bevilaqua lives on Crescent Beach in Saint Augustine with her son, Alessandro. Her poems have been published in or accepted for future publication by Atticus Review, Apogee Journal, Tupelo Quarterly, Kentucky Review, Menacing Hedge, Construction, here/there, Iodine Poetry Journal, Hubbub, Houseboat, and other publications. She is the author of **Holding Breath: A Memoir of AIDS' Wildfire Days**, and will be publishing a poetry chapbook entitled **Gospel** in the near future.

Chris Bodor relocated from New York to Saint Augustine in 2003 after working for ten years in NY City. In August of 2009, Chris started hosting monthly poetry open mic readings on the last Sunday of every month, under the name Ancient City Poets. The name was created by Glenda Bailey-Mershon for a series of 2009 National Poetry Month events. Chris runs his own imprint, Poet Plant Press, with his wife Mary Beth. He has also revived his journalism career by shooting pictures and writing pieces for Old City Life, the St. Augustine Record and other national publications.

Pris Campbell, a former Clinical Psychologist, arrived in South Florida in the late seventies after a meandering six month trip from Boston in her 22 foot sailboat with her cat Monster and her now ex. Her love of warm weather and the colorful Florida sea kept her there. Hobbled by ME/CFS since 1990, the sound of surf and the scent of salt air rejuvenate her soul, feed her creativity.

Lance Carden moved to St. Augustine in 2013, after a career in journalism at The Christian Science Monitor. He has written a book of poems to celebrate the city's 450th anniversary in 2015. Last year, he and his wife, C.M.L. Vincent, published **Tuscan Retreat**, poems that chronicle a two-month visit to Italy in 2011. Lance is also author of **Witness: An Oral History of Black Politics in Boston, 1920 to 1960**.

Alan Catlin lives in Schenectady, New York and has been publishing for parts of five decades. During that time he has published over sixty chapbooks and full length books of prose and poetry. His latest full length book, the gender bending memoir, **Books of the Dead: a memoir with poetry** as well as a forthcoming chapbook of poetry from Night Ballet Press, **Beautiful Mutants**.

"Charlie Cawley sees things most don't." were words written by a viewer of his photographs. His response to that was "It's this life that makes the art, on all days, and in all ways. I just try to keep the camera handy for the times when I SEE it. There are in this life those times when the camera clicks, and I say 'Thank you!'" Charlie is seeking a publisher for his new book **Scene: St. Augustine**, hopefully to be published in 2015 to correspond with St. Augustine's 450th year as America's Oldest City.

Stevie Cenko was born under a trailer with her two brothers in Fruitland Park, Florida.

David Dannov graduated from CSULB's creative writing program in 1994 under the direction of Gerald Locklin. Since then, he went on a pilgrimage into the world of words, eventually becoming a novelist. After decades of odd jobs in America, now teaching English overseas, he's finished eight novels, a shorty story collection, and seven narrative poetry books. He feels he's finally arrived.

John De Herrera is a writer/artist who lives and works in Santa Barbara, California. He is author of the novel **The Kingsnake in the Sun**, and **Hamlet/Macbeth: Translations**. He is currently working on his second novel.

Mary Deno-Yeck has been a resident of Saint Augustine since 2010. She is a transplant from Millbrook, NY, where she previously lived for thirty years. She has always had an interest in history and the natural sciences, and finds that writing about Florida gives her the opportunity to combine those interests.

Explaining that Jim Draper was born in Kosciusko, Mississippi in 1953 says a lot about his attitude toward story telling. He studied art in college and has worked as a painter for most of his adult life. Jacksonville, Florida has been his home for the last twenty years. Frustration with his being able to tell stories effectively using only a paint brush led him to the Shantyboat writing workshops.

Brian Druggan lives in Reynoldsburg, Ohio with his wife and daughter. He has recently begun exploring his love of photography. His favorite city to photograph is Saint Augustine, Florida where he hopes to retire sooner rather than later.

Dan Florez, a native of the East Coast, was raised on the Outer Banks of North Carolina. He is a graduate of Flagler College with a Fine Arts degree with emphasis on painting and traditional darkroom photography and he currently resides in Saint Augustine. Since graduation, he's freelanced for a variety of publications, documented weddings, and established photography procedures at marine mammal interaction facilities.

Tim Gilmore is the author of several books, including **In Search of Eartha White, Storehouse for the People**, **The Ocean Highway at Night**, and **Stalking Ottis Toole: A Southern Gothic**. Because he finds Florida teeming with the Southern Gothic once you peel back the pastel paint, he explores and writes about it at www.jaxpsychogeo.com. He teaches Literature and Composition at Florida State College of Jacksonville. His writings have appeared in several local and national publications.

Lou Graves is the author of **there is an emptiness**, a collection of poetry. He has been published in Out Of Our, The Write Room, My Favorite Bullet, and others. When not writing he can be found reading in the corner of a dark bar. He lives in Saint Augustine, Florida with his cat Vito.

Lynn Skapyak Harlin is a poet who made her living by selling her words as a freelance writer, photographer, and newspaper reporter. Her first published poem "War Waste" appeared in Time magazine, in 1970. Her poems have appeared in State Street Review, Arbus magazine, Section Eight Magazine, Aquarian, deadpaper.org and many others. Her two chap books, **Real Women Drive Trucks** and **Press One for More Options** were published in 1997 by Closet Books.

Tovah Janovsky lives and writes in Palm Coast and loves "all things Florida". Having returned from a cross-country train trip, her notebook is hip deep in poems and stories which she will post on her blog.tovahsez.wordpress.com.

Leny Kaltenekker is a retired nurse who writes in both English and Dutch. She is known as an "occasional poet" because she often writes poems for friends for their birthday and other special occasions. She lives in Saint Augustine, Florida.

Jane Lynahan Karklin is a graduate of the American Academy of Dramatic Arts in New York City. She has published four books of poetry and her writings have also appeared in a variety of poetry anthologies. Jane and her husband, David, reside in Sarasota, Florida.

Raised on the water in New York and Maine, photographer LeeAnn Kendall loves the outdoors and everything to do with water life. She lives in Saint Augustine Beach, Florida and is usually on the beach, camera in hand, at sunrise.

Beverly A. Bell Kessler is a self-taught writer who has written for more than 50 years. Raised in Maryland and educated at the New York Institute of Finance, Beverly had a thirty year career as a Sr. Vice President, Stock Broker and Full Financial Advisor with Merrill Lynch and Wachovia

Securities. She retired in 2000 and in 2006 she and her husband Robert started a Mitigation Banking Company, Environment Heritage Investors, LLC which represents both of their careers. Beverly has published some of her poems and she hope to publish her book **For the Benefit of Ivy**. Her book is a lyrical autobiography of her experiences, opinions and philosophies. Her inspiration came from her great-great grandmother.

Ann Kiyonaga-Razon received a master's degree from the Johns Hopkins School of Advanced International Studies (SAIS). Shortly after receiving this degree, she had the great, good fortune to spend over a decade in an ashram (monastery). She has written a book of poems entitled **Flight into the Dawn - a Collection of Poems Celebrating Life's Moments** and has taught a poetry course, facilitated poetry gatherings at the local Barnes and Noble and held poetry workshops. She lives with her family in the beautiful town of Saint Augustine, Florida.

Rachel Layne is a massage therapist, dancer and yoga instructor with a passion for self-expression in all forms. She enjoys writing and believes it can be therapeutic for the soul.

Dotty Loop is a native North Floridian, so she writes with a Southern voice. Since retirement from teaching in 2002, she writes both poetry and prose. It is usually humorous. Halloween is her favorite holiday. She recently dressed up like Virginia Woolf.

Susan Bennett Lopez is an established visual and spoken word artist whose work has been published in FM Summer 2013, Words, Drift Quarterly: Motion Means Everything, Dialogue Among Civilizations Through Poetry: United Nations Poetry & Prose Anthology (2001), ABCTales.com and Writers, Inc. One of her more notable performances includes the Spirit Lowell Celebrates Kerouac live poetry CD recorded in Lowell, MA in 2001. Spoken word performances venues include Nuyorican Poets Cafe, The Knitting Factory, St. Mark's Poetry Project, The Bitter End, The Living Room, The Salon, C-Note and The Elbow Room in NYC. She currently resides in Tennessee with her family, where in addition to writing; she spends her time creating Modern Vintage designs for her company LuckyGirlEleven.com.

Gayl *Angela* Masson is a Saint Augustine filmmaker, writer and artist. She works in digital film, traditional paints, graphics, and text, revealing color in words and words in color. More of her work can be found at www.JetLady.com.

Ann Browning Masters is the author of **Floridanos, Menorcans, Cattle-Whip Crackers**. Poetry from this collection has been published in anthologies and journals, read at the Marjorie Kinnan Rawlings Annual Conference and Florida Literary Arts Coalition Conference, recognized at the Florida Folk Festival, and recorded for the Florida State Historical Archives. Recently retired as a faculty member at St. Johns River State College, she continues to read from her work in the Eckerd College Road Scholar Program. A Saint Augustine native, Dr. Masters is a 12th generation Floridian.

Bozena Helena Mazur-Nowak comes from Opole (Poland). She lives near London (UK). Verses author, translated by herself into English, published in the U.S, Canada, India, Australia, Africa. and the UK. He work is simple and accessible, but lyrical and well crafted. She has published five books of poetry. Most recently, **Blue Longing** was published in Canada in 2014.

Mischele Miller is photographer and writer. She enjoys writing poetry and short stories and has written a play, "A Price to Pay", that she hopes will be produced. Mischele spent much of her childhood in Saint Augustine, enjoying the ocean and sunshine and much of her writing takes place in various locations in Florida, including her poem, "Hurricane Winds". Mischele is currently working on completing her first novel.

Tonn Pastore lives and works at the beach. He is the author of **Convergence**, a poetry collection published by Closet Books in 2003.

Lee Patterson is a teacher and writer originally from Miami, Florida. His work has been published in the Columbia Review, West 10th, and in anthologies from Poet Plant Press and Dagda Publishing.

Bob Patterson is a singer / songwriter / storyteller / author / photographer / environmentalist. Additionally, he is a recipient of "The Fellow Man and Mother Earth Award" from the Stetson Kennedy Foundation and, a Lifetime Achievement Award from the Florida Storytelling Association. He has numerous songwriting awards including "Best Florida Song". He is a Co-Founder of the Gamble Rogers festival where he serves as the event's Artistic Director.

Becky Meyer Pourchot is the author of the **Hungry Ghost Series** and **I Look Better in Binary**, a compilation of childhood mishaps. She is also the author of **Forgive Me Martha**, a collection of irreverent poems written to none other than the Great Goddess of Domesticity herself: Martha Stewart.

Nadia Ramoutar was born in Dublin, Ireland surrounded by mountains, oceans and incredible poet's legacies at every turn. She immigrated to America as a teenager with her West Indian Father and Irish Mother. A lifelong writer and seeker, Nadia holds a Ph. D in Communication from University of Florida. A filmmaker, college professor, writer and inspirational speaker, she lives in Saint Augustine, Florida with her two sons.

Kathleen (Ramiccio) Roberts has been writing poetry since she was 11 years old and was awakened by the full moon shining in her bedroom window. Although she writes of many things, the full moon is her main source of inspiration. You can bet that every full moon she will be out there dancing and writing.

Rebecca Rousseau is an abstract and expressionist artist. Her abstraction is simple and organic and built from bold, energetic colors. Her inspiration is influenced by the aesthetic traditions of Haiti, Mexico, and southern California, and she takes inspiration from the rich East Coast art culture where she lives.

Kimmy Van Kooten, first and foremost is a wife and mother of 11 children. She has been inspired by her journey from her birth place in New Jersey to Pennsylvania, where she and her 15 siblings resided on a seventy acre horse farm. In 1994 she and her children moved to Saint Augustine from Daytona Beach. Kimmy now attends Flagler College, pursuing her lifelong dream of obtaining her BFA in Fine Arts. In her spare time she illustrates children's books, book covers, and writes poetry. She also might be found downtown playing on her red conga drums.

Her collection, **Peace of Language** (Avenue U, 2013), features many of her playful, spirited poems as well as several of her inspiring illustrations

Marie Vernon is author or co-author of published works that include regional histories Speaking of Our Past and The Garrison Church; novel **Graceland Express**; True Crime stories **Deadly Lust and Deadly Charm**; and mystery novel, **Above Fold**. Her articles, columns and book reviews have appeared in numerous publications. She lives in Saint Augustine.

Rob Waldner fell in love with poetry as a teenager when he first began to seriously explore his writing abilities. A self-proclaimed freestyle poet, his most recent work is inspired by his family, the world around him, and the elements in life which affect him the most on a personal level. Rob lives in Palm Coast, Florida with his wife and three young children.

Lee Weaver is a playwright and actor who lives with his wife in Saint Augustine, Florida. Many historians say that whereas the events of Montgomery Alabama sent the Civil Rights Legislation to Congress, the city of Saint Augustine moved it to President Lyndon Johnson's desk for signing. Weaver's most recent play, "The Witness," tells of the national Civil Rights struggle and specifically, the struggle in Saint Augustine. One of the events of paramount importance in the struggle is called "The Crossing." It speaks of the time Andrew Young, an African American clergyman, who went on to become a Congressman, Ambassador to the United Nations and Mayor of Atlanta, Ga., was sent to Saint Augustine in 1963, by Dr. Martin Luther King Jr. In Saint Augustine, Young was assaulted by an angry mob of racists in the town square, the Plaza de la Constitution, where slave auctions once took place. This event played a critical part in the forward movement of the struggle. Weaver's poem, "My Maggie," a reflection from "The Witness," is in the voice of Beauregard Lee, a racist who participated in the assault.

Beem Weeks is a 40-something-year-old author of several short stories, poems, essays, and the historical fiction/coming-of-age novel **Jazz Baby**. A divorced father of two grown children, Beem has lived in Florida and Georgia, and is currently calling Michigan home. Among his literary influences he counts Daniel Woodrell, Barbara Kingsolver, and Stephen Geez. His latest release is a collection of short stories entitled **Slivers of Life**.

Ginna Wilkerson completed a Ph.D. in Creative Writing at University of Aberdeen in 2013, also the year of publication of her first poetry collection, Odd Remains. She received a 2012 Poetry Kit Award for the poem 'Dimensions'. Currently, she teaches writing at Ringling College of Art and Design.